Raifen

Raifen
THE SEARCH FOR TRUTH

MATTHEW THRUSH

TATE PUBLISHING & *Enterprises*

Published by Tate Publishing & Enterprises, LLC
127 E. Trade Center Terrace | Mustang, Oklahoma 73064 USA
1.888.361.9473 | www.tatepublishing.com

Tate Publishing is committed to excellence in the publishing industry. The company reflects the philosophy established by the founders, based on Psalm 68:11,
"The Lord gave the word and great was the company of those who published it."

Book design copyright © 2008 by Tate Publishing, LLC. All rights reserved.
Cover & interior design by Lynly D. Taylor
Cover art by Kevin P. Thrush

Published in the United States of America
ISBN: 978-1-60462-995-8
1. Fiction: Action & Adventure   2. Fiction: Fantasy: Series

08.07.16

TABLE OF CONTENTS

INTRODUCTION

In the darkness of night a creature lurks behind a bush. A snap of a twig is the only sound possible to comprehend. This creature, this human destroyer, brings nothing but pain, anxiety; it brings death. It is known as exactly that, "the Bringer of Death." Many still do not know the real true form of this hazardous being, but the ones who have seen its movement, never are seen again. Rumors indicate once someone senses it near them, they get consumed by the beast. Of course, it's just a rumor, but a considerably believable one. For once someone said they thought they felt something, they would just disappear that very night. No one is quite sure what this thing is that seems, by the tell-tales, to come and take the unworthy people to be its slaves. Or that is if it deems them worthy to serve as slaves, if not, no one is sure what happens to them. Most likely the particles of nourishment for the Bringer of Death's army and the minions that make its ranks: nasty bloodthirsty Fangoers, Talions, and creatures from the dark worlds. No one knows quite how to stop the un-killable creature, but one's fate may have and be the only hope mankind has left. Over the years a group of people called the Nazracs came and landed on our eastern shore. They came from a place called Petipala, somewhere in the south. With their help, the ancestors were able to hold out against the Bringer of Death and his trusted advisors and adversaries. But, how long can we keep this up? Not long enough. There has to be someone, something, in this ghastly world that can destroy the Bringer of Death. An answer still not found, until now.

Raifen

THE SEARCH FOR TRUTH

PART ONE: TRUTH

PRELUDE

In a valley far from any worries, there lives a young boy—a young man in the standard of the day, but in his late teens. His name, Raifen, means one who hopes or brings hope; one who believes everything happens for a reason. The entire world's fate lies in this young man's unknowing hands. If he fails, the inevitable will happen. The world will fall into a darkness it has never seen nor dreamt of. If he succeeds, the life and the way things used to be when the ancestors lived will come back in effect, and hope will be restored to the races. How can all this expectation lie on one young man? Little does he or anyone else know of his great fate and hidden talents. On this morning, cool and crisp, five hundred years since the war first started, young Raifen wakes up and starts his chores. He lives with his uncle, helping with the farm. After his mother died giving birth to him and his father left, he became one without a family. His mother's will was for her brother to look after him if anything happened to her. So, his uncle became his father figure. It has since been for seventeen years to the day. Most was kept secret about his parents all this time, but some things can never stay hidden forever.

There he sat all alone in the corner. Not a single soul was near. Not a single voice could be heard. Each person who passed did not even notice his figure hunched over

MATTHEW THRUSH

itself in the shadows. He knew how he must remain silent so that no one would see him. He knew how to remain unheard, unseen, unfelt, and unknown. He had been doing so for the past few months now, ever since he first was put in *there*. He couldn't help the shudder that found his skin. If he were not careful, he could be caught. That would not be a good idea. He knew the last thing he wanted was to go back to the asylum, the place of sins and people's hell. He never knew why he was there himself, but one thing was certain, he never was going back. He would kill anyone who would dare try and make him. He had vowed this to himself upon escape. His plan had been so perfect, so sly and masterful that he didn't know he had been capable of such a task. He smiled to himself inwardly. Of course he was skilled enough. He had escaped unnoticed, unhinged, un-abided, and unscathed, hadn't he? Yes, he had. And there would be much more time for him to put his skills into more *dangerous* tasks.

The child picked himself up off the floor slowly, as not to make any unneeded motions to draw attention. He had scoped the place out for days now, memorizing the movements, the customers, the clerk and the shelves of potions, books, toys, antiques, and many other neat things as well. Some of which were not as interesting as the one thing he now wanted. It was in the same place as it had been a few days earlier when he had first spotted it. It had been there the following ten days afterward, too, as he had noticed. As the days went by, he snuck in the same small little hole in the back of the building. It was a shallow crack in the wall and was covered up well by an overhanging piece of sign that had long since lost its balance and strength on the outside street wall. Apparently it had been thrown in the side alley by the owner of the place. It had been out placed by a newer more detailed sign. But the beauty of it didn't really matter to him. All he needed was to hide his entrance and exit. He made sure no one followed him into the alley, too, each and every time he did so. He would sit there, in the far corner of the alley, in the shadows and wait. Sometimes he would wait for hours before daring to go into the hole. But as the days went by, he became more daring and courageous and soon he rarely stayed a few minutes before going in. He had become so sure of himself and his skills that he did not believe someone could fol- low him. And if by some miracle they did, they would find themselves trapped in a dead end. And then their time would be up. The boy would make sure of it. But, fortunate for the person who followed, unfortunate for him not being able to inflict the pain he wanted, no one had even come close. Once, another boy had tried to follow but soon gave up, finding himself utterly lost in the forests that he would go through before getting to his final destination. That was all preparation for what the real task was. It was nothing to just be careful; to not get caught was a greater reason. He wanted it and it wanted him.

The boy waited for the clerk to walk to the back as he had always done before at the exact time to tend to some boxes. Once the man was gone, the boy waited just a few seconds to make sure all was clear. Slowly, he crept out of his hiding place of darkness. He stayed crouched just in case someone else was in the room with him or the man surprisingly came back sooner than expected. Neither happened; yet. The boy snuck around the counter, now standing exactly in front of the door of which the man had exited. If the clerk came back now he would find him standing there. That would not be a pleasing sight. The boy grabbed a small stool and climbed up on it. He was not very tall at his age of twelve years, so he needed to use this miniature ladder to get to his treasure. He now stood about ten feet off the ground, not counting his reaching hands. He strained to reach at the small object he had come for, but he couldn't reach it. His fingers failed to touch even the outskirts of the object. The boy cursed to himself for being so stupid. He was about to give up and leave, since he had already taken way too much time, but stopped his departure. He thought he had heard something. He brushed it aside and started climbing back down again. But there it was again, this time a little louder. The boy looked around the room, peering over all the shelves looking for the source of this voice. There was no one in the store. As was expected, but the boy couldn't help but feel curious as to what was making the noise. He remained there for a few more seconds then decided to leave.

"Here."

The boy looked around at the sudden yell. He had

almost fallen off the stool from the last blast. He spun around on the stool to where his face was facing the shelf that held the object he had come for. Yet, the sound seemed to be coming from a far distant place. As if it were in another realm or plain.

"Here."

This time the boy looked straight at the location of the voice. But there was nothing there. Feeling stupid and a little uncomfortable, the boy kept an eye on that spot. As his eyes continued their probing they shot open, springing to life. There was something in between two boxes, in the dark crevice that they formed. He couldn't be sure, but he thought there to be something glowing. He thought his eyes were playing tricks on him but then there it was again, the same spark of light. It was only a split second that the boy thought he could have been mistaken. He climbed down and moved the stool over to the right a few feet, then climbed back up. The black hole loomed just above him, or actually it was only a few inches away. If he stood on his tippy-toes, and he did so, his face hovered parallel to the spot. Not a few inches away the voice spoke again, but not as loudly as it had done earlier. The boy almost thought he was hearing things. If it had not been for him being right next to it, he might have never heard it.

"Here, take it, take it. Take me. Here…"

The boy peered harder into the darkness. Again there came the blinking of some kind of light. The boy did not flinch. He reached up his right hand, feeling for anything that might be in between the boxes. At first there was nothing and his mood sank. He began to pull his hand away, but touched something.

"Here."

He grabbed around at the object that his finger had touched and soon found a hold. He slowly drew it out of its cubbyhole and into the light. His eyes lit up to the glow of the sun. In his hands he held something of such beauty he knew not what it could have been. The small rectangular box shimmered in the air. A soft glow sparkled, beating every now and then with a shock of light.

"Here."

The boy quickly climbed down the stool. He stashed his new gift into his pocket and hurriedly made way to leave. He had just barely gotten out from behind the counter when the clerk came back. The clerk looked surprised to see him there. His look of surprise soon turned from shock to one of suspicion.

"Can I help you?" the clerk asked, coming around the counter.

The boy did not answer and instead began to walk briskly around the shelves. The man saw the boy's pace quicken and in response his voice became more urgent.

"Can I help you young man?" he asked again, but not really expecting the boy to answer. He just was using it as an excuse to come after him, though in truth he really didn't need one. The boy was now a few feet from his hiding place when he bolted towards the hole. The man saw this and leapt at him. The clerk's hands missed the boy by a hair. The boy quickly scurried through the hole and out into the alley. He knew the clerk would not follow, could not, to be more precise. The hole was too small, another reason why the boy liked it so much. He smiled to himself. He felt for the object he had just stolen. The smooth edges coaxed him with a deep satisfaction. He had done well. He walked away. He did not look back once as he left. He did not care that he would never be back here again. The hole had sufficed him for what he needed; now he had no use for it. Besides, the clerk was sure to board it up now. The boy smiled inwardly. The boy disappeared back into the trees at the end of the alleyway, all the while his hand still in his pocket.

MEMORIES OF VLANDRAX XEN

An Awakening

And so it shall come to pass that one will come and walk among us that can change the world. His presence shall be known among few, but he shall still be within our grasps. We shall never know who, what, or where he is going or where he went. His destiny is his to choose. He shall have a choice, one that shall hold a barrier to truth and life. If he accepts the gift, he shall be holy. If he rejects it, he shall be lost. There are many times ahead for him. He shall need to pay heed to what lies before him, for if he concentrates too fully on the past, he shall lose himself within their sins. Free from all hands. Free from sin. Free from lies. And free to make his own decisions. He is coming. All shall lay their lives in his hands. He must decide how to accept. A choice wavers on the horizon. What will it be...

From the Scrolls of Deracy

The morning was cool and still shallow with the night billowing like rain clouds over the sky. It wrapped its hands around the land, cascading the features of the trees and mountains into glimpses of shadow and mystery. All was unseen, all was unheard, and all was un-happening; at least that's what it looked like. Through the darkness, somewhere off in the distance, a destiny was being fulfilled. Young Raifen woke up shortly before the early morning calls of wakefulness. He scampered off into his clothes and went out to tend to the animals. It was an everyday occurrence for him, waking up early, before the sun had a chance to catch up with the darkness, to feed the animals. He quickly poured food for the goats, the sheep, the cows, and the horses, then he headed to the chicken coop. It was always eventful whenever he would go into the chicken pen to deal with the chickens. They were a wild bunch and they rarely allowed for him to get their eggs without a fight. As Raifen walked briskly across the expanse of ground between where the horses were settled and the chicken house was, his fingers wiggled anxiously. He clutched his knuckles, cracking them together. A grin spread across his lips as he neared the door. He stopped just before the door a few feet away. He remained silent and listened. The chickens seemed to be asleep still. He grinned again. And without further ado he lunged in on the supposedly sleeping chickens.

Upon entering the chicken house Raifen was surprised to see the chickens were all awake. Hundreds of small white eyes peered at him in the darkness of the shed. He hesitated, and then continued. He went for the nearest chicken and tried to reach under her to get at the eggs she no doubt had produced over the night. But just as he was a few inches away, the entire shed cascaded into a riot. All the chickens flew at him all at once. Raifen tried to shield himself from them but he was unable to do so completely. His arms, ears, legs, and every other part of his body were now being nibbled on. He screamed in agony and brushed them aside. He kicked and flared his arms violently. He managed to knock a few chickens off of him, but it didn't last long before ten more took their place. Raifen decided it was a lost cause and quickly fumbled through and grabbed as many eggs as he could. A few minutes later and he was

MATTHEW THRUSH

standing back outside the shed, covered in feathers and bleeding from several places. He brushed himself off and admired his few treasures he had managed to escape with. Six eggs lay in his basket. Raifen sighed with displeasure. Another day had gone by and he still hadn't managed to procure a decent quantity of eggs. The battle was over and he had lost again. But he had faith; the war wasn't over just yet. Raifen was walking off back to the house but stopped. His head was bent forward just a little. His eyes radiated with an inner excitement. He had thought of a way to get back at them. He laid the basket of eggs on the ground right where he stood and turned back around. He stomped off in the direction of the shed. He wasn't through with them just yet. He grinned all the more with pleasure. He would have his revenge, and his unsuspecting prey would not even know what hit them until after it was over. Raifen reached the shed and instead of going inside he circled around and went to another small house not ten feet away.

He bent down over the little miniature home and whispered, "Bestrow."

He heard a whimper from inside and knew the old hound was asleep. He called him again, this time a little louder. The hound shifted and opened an eye. Raifen smiled.

"Hey boy, want to have some fun?" Raifen smiled all the more. His dog looked at him confused. All he wanted was to be left alone and sleep. But today he wouldn't have that leisure. Today he would get a chance at something he had always wanted to do. Raifen reached in and grabbed Bestrow by the ears. He gently dragged him out of his sleeping quarters and pet him on the head. Raifen bent down and put his face against the hounds. Bestrow's tired looking eyes shot open with energy and excitement. Raifen stood back up and smiled again. He turned around and walked back to the shed. He was in front of the shed now and he stood there, pondering what was about to transpire. He might get in trouble from his uncle, but he could deal with that. Besides, the chickens needed to learn who was boss. He looked down at his old hound again.

"Ready boy?"

Bestrow licked his face and if a dog could smile, he was doing so with the biggest one ever. Raifen went up to the door and gripped the handle.

"Go get 'em boy!" he shouted and he opened the door. Instantly Bestrow shot forward and disappeared into the chicken house. The sound of chaos echoed from within the shed's walls. Raifen smiled to himself.

"That'll teach you," he said to himself, but more to the unhearing chickens. He turned around and walked away. He would allow Bestrow a few minutes of glory and fun before taking him out again. Raifen went back and picked up the basket of eggs and brought them inside the house. He came back out a few moments later and walked back to the shed. He waited a few moments then opened the door. He whistled and Bestrow came trotting out. Raifen burst out laughing. His hound was covered entirely with feathers. His dog didn't even look like a dog anymore. Raifen couldn't contain himself and he tumbled to the ground laughing, tears rolling from his eyes. Bestrow grinned and shook, trying to free himself of the feathers. Raifen got

MATTHEW THRUSH

a hold of himself shortly and helped his poor dog clean himself. After all the feathers were off, he sat there with his dog. He patted his head and scratched behind his ears. Bestrow moaned with pleasure.

"Good boy," confided Raifen and Bestrow smiled knowingly. Raifen smiled but then stopped suddenly. He looked around trying to see who had spoken, but there was no one around. Raifen thought it was strange but then decided it was just the wind blowing through the trees. He stood up and walked over to his favorite spot of hang out. He entered the edges of the forest and sat beneath his favorite tree. He had named it a few years back when he had first discovered its secret. He turned around and checked to make sure no one was watching then quickly climbed up into the tree. Raifen was a natural climber and quickly accelerated to the innermost location in the tree's branches. He placed himself on a large round branch, and lied against the trunk base of the tree. He was completely covered and shielded from anything outside. He was in a completely fortified fortress. The leaves and thick expanse of tree branches provided for the deep shelter. Raifen oftentimes would come here and just sit and listen to the forest. Rain could not get in where he was either. He had been stuck out in the forest once when it was storming and he had needed shelter, so he climbed up his secret hideout and lay inside until the storm had passed. His uncle had been worried about him and had pleaded for him to tell him where he was, but Raifen refused. All he said was that he was with Tibit. His uncle had asked repeatedly who Tibit was but Raifen had never told. The truth was Tibit wasn't anyone; it was his secret location, his tree. Raifen peered at the spot where he had carved the name so many years ago. The name had just come to him then, as if the tree had told him itself. Raifen had obliged and etched the name into the bark. It still held its shape even after seven years of age wearing at its edges. It appeared the name stuck and would remain there forever. Raifen liked the idea. He closed his eyes and allowed his mind to spin to another world, his imagination.

Raifen submerged into a plain of invisible life. He went there often but this time something was different. Someone else was there with him, at least he didn't feel alone this time. He didn't bother with it and continued his daydreaming. Before he knew it, hours had gone by. He would not have woken up from his sleep if he hadn't heard it. His eyes shot open. He looked around, but nothing was there. He still was in the cubbyhole of Tibit. He sat there breathing somewhat hard. He had a little perspiration on his skin and his shirt felt damp. It had been a cool morning so he couldn't understand why he was sweating. It wasn't hot in the tree either. This confused him. He shifted to get to the area where he would enter and exit at but stopped. He heard it again. This time he knew he had heard something. He peered around in the shadows of the branches but could not see anything. He brushed it aside again and began climbing down. He halted again in his departure. He quickly climbed back up into the tree. He sat there at the entrance, absorbing the entire picture of the inside. Every light, every shadow, every leaf, every branch and every single thing that could be noted, the smell, taste, and feel. Nothing caught

MATTHEW THRUSH

his attention, but he knew not to believe the oblivious, the hair on the back of his neck was still standing. Something or someone was there, he just didn't know where. He hesitated a few seconds more, then climbed down rapidly. He leaped the last few feet to the ground and ran off.

He made it to the shed of chickens before he dared to look back. The forest was just as it always was, with his hiding place on the edge. Something had happened, he just didn't know what. He had an uneasy feeling he was being watched. He went to the barn and continued his morning chores. The sun was now up and he could hear the first calls of life on the farm. Tending to the gathering of hay and cleaning up manure allowed for his mind to escape the mysterious presence in Tibit, something he was grateful for.

While Raifen was tending to the horses again and cleaning up the barn his uncle walked in. Raifen looked up to see his uncle walk in. He smiled.

"Hi, Uncle Seraph!"

His uncle scolded.

"How many times do I have to tell you not to call me Uncle, just call me Seraph, please," stated Seraph more than asking. Raifen grinned.

"As many times as need be until I learn." His uncle frowned.

"I'll be sure to from now on." Raifen smiled again and reached the pitchfork deep into a pile of hay and hauled it in the air and placed it on a pile in front of one of the horses' pins. He continuously made this mistake to frustrate his uncle.

"Is there something you needed?" asked Raifen on a more serious note. His laughter subsided in his mind when he noticed his uncle looked a bit shook up, seemingly pale-colored in the face as if he were a spirit come back from the dead to curse the souls of the earth. A rough, couple day in the making, batch of hair curled around his chin. Even his clothes were noticeably extra dirty than they usually would be. Raifen knew his uncle not to have worked any harder or any longer than usual, so the thought of where the dirt had come from shook a foul note in his thoughts. Until he realized of course that it was not just one day's work, but that of a week's worth. His uncle was still wearing the same clothing of the week before. A look of confusion and terror alighted in his eyes. Also, it appeared that a tear had manifested itself a home under one of them; those blue, crystalloid eyes born with much wisdom from his old age. Though a little hesitant at first, he finally begins to respond, "I'm afraid there is Raifen."

Raifen stood stunned in a silenced anticipation.

"I have had an awful dream this past night." His Uncle looked at him, deeply into his nephew's face. Raifen could tell his uncle was terrified about something. The sparks of white lightning in his eyes gave it away.

"I dreamt that this curtain of darkness came. People were screaming and running around as if they had their heads cut off. Some literally did. Kids were crying, houses were either burning or were already burned to ashes, and Talions and Fangors were spilling blood everywhere they

MATTHEW THRUSH

went. Just killing one after the other, heedless of their crying pleas. Thousands upon thousands of them." replied Seraph, reliving the nightmare once more.

A Talion was a large, but rather squat-looking kind of creature. It had one eye in the center of its head. It was told that the one eye could see better than two. Though none have been able to prove this, it is still believed to this day. Their kills were swift and gruesome. They would not allow any to survive. The Fangor was the brethren of the Talion. Similar to its kin, it too had one eye located on its forehead, but looking closely you could see another smaller one, almost invisible parallel to the first. This one was supposed to be a special eye. It could see through things as if nothing was ever there. Unlike its brother who had smaller teeth for pincers, the Fangor had large fangs that drooped over its bottom lip, forming a deadly bite. The Fangor was also much bigger than the Talion. While the Talion was swift and quick in its movements, the Fangor was slower, but more vicious in battle. The Fangor would rely on brute force over tactical warfare. Each was deadly by itself, but if you had the unlucky fortune to cross the pair, you might as well have been dead in the first place. Their combined battle fury was unknown of. And people were terrified of these new, unseen beasts. They caused great havoc and destruction before people began to take courage and fight against them. They were the infantry of a vast and great army. Though one would think they were the special weapons of death, they were not. They were used to cause fear and to wreak death to whatever they touched. And they did so, and were the best at carrying out their gifts. The gift of death.

"Don't worry about it, Uncle. I'm sure it was nothing, just a bad dream," sympathized Raifen, trying to comfort his uncle.

"But," started Seraph, "I have been having this dream for awhile now, but never this clear and dreadful before. As if I were there and it was really happening. More or less the past or the future to come. Do you see what I am trying to say?" asked Seraph.

"I'm sure it was nothing, Uncle, don't bother yourself with it." Raifen knew there was more to this little dream his uncle had, but he decided it best to not dwell on the subject. Besides, focusing too much on the negative can have a negative output in your life. No need for any unneeded stress to come his way, or especially to his uncle. His uncle did not listen though and instead kept on in his rebukes of the dream.

"But it does bother me Raifen."

Raifen did not understand why his uncle was so worked up. Why would it matter if he had a bad dream? Besides, it was a dream after all, wasn't it? Seraph continued, unknowing of his nephew's assumptions, "It was coming after you."

Seraph seemed to be getting even more worked up now. His hands went flailing about in motions to show what he was trying to get across.

"More like you were running towards it. As if you could somehow stop it. Even if trying was of no use." A horror-stricken feeling ran down Raifen's spine, he felt cold and wet with fear. If this was truly what his Uncle had been dreaming, Raifen thought to himself, then maybe it was real.

Raifen changed his mind about his uncle exaggerating the situation. Something was tugging at the back of his mind. When he remembered what it was, it was all he could do not to join his uncle in lamentation.

But how and *why* his uncle too? He looked up at his uncle with a different outlook. He respected this man. His uncle is so wise and so brave. He was not afraid of showing his emotions, which Raifen thought men should not do. No, his uncle was a real man, courageous and full of bravery and wisdom. Raifen did not think he had any of these attributes. But he hoped one day to attain them as his uncle had, some through pain, some through pleasure.

Through the stifled cries of worry from his uncle's lip, Raifen remembered what had caused him alarm when realizing the enormity of the situation at hand. Not that it was anything really to fret about, but something that needed some more consideration and time to understand fully. Raifen then thought to himself, remembering the nights before when he, too, had been having dreams like the ones his uncle was referring to. The same kind of dreams had harvested in his mind at night. All those sleepless nights, going to waste. Rest was not something Raifen had experienced in a few weeks. And it showed, though he tried to hide it, with fake movements and comments and actions whenever his uncle was around.

What could it mean, thought Raifen. What secrets possibly were being held from him? Would he ever know?

Or would he remain oblivious to the truth and never really find meaning behind his dreams and thoughts? He meant to find out.

"Uncle?" he asked, ready to get answers. "I have been having dreams similar to the ones that bind you."

Seraph looked up, almost as if he were waking up for the first time in a long time. His eyes returned to their normal color, but not for much longer.

"The memory is faint in my mind but, I do remember ..."

The room was dark and quiet. A faint whisper of the wind rasped its arms against the boundaries of the house. The house too was deathly quiet. A gentle gleam of light peeked its face in through the window and found its rest on the bed. The figure lay there unmoving and unknowing of his sneaky guest. In the other rooms the same darkness loomed and made its sanctuary. None could pass through unless granted permission, none except this tiny particle of light could.

The figure lying on the bed moved in his sleep. To an untrained eye one would think him merely sleeping. To the wise, it was more. The small ray of light shifted and returned to the window. Before departing back to where it had come from, it sparked, and then vanished. The room was left dark. The figure snapped up from his sleep. His breathing was shallow but clearly unnatural. He peered around the room anxiously, almost longing for something to show itself to him. Nothing did. The figure moved to unwrap the blankets from his body and his feet fell to the floor. His face cringed from the coldness that still lingered on its solid surface. He sat there on the edge of his bed, peering through the haze of darkness. Something had awakened him from his sleep but he didn't know what. A weird silence blanketed him. He could hear the wind howling outside, the trees fighting off the urge to fly with it, remaining firm in its structure. Leaves cascaded from the treetops and pounded against the walls of the house, some bits and pieces smashing into the window. The figure turned suddenly towards the solemn window in his bed chamber. He stared at the display of leaves splashing its surface. Slowly, he stood and walked over to it and glimpsed out. His mind twirled with curiosity at the sight of blue clouds dripping its tentacles down out of the sky and overshadowing the forest, working its way to him. Fear and adrenaline electrified his nerves. He quickly put on some trousers and shoes and went to the front door. It was quiet in the house until he opened the door. The wind rushed in and threatened to smash him into the wall but he fought it off vigorously. He squeezed himself through the door and pulled it shut. Now outside, the world was completely changed. Chaos ruled and noise draped everything but there was still a calmness about it. Unlike inside where it was warm and quiet, outside it was ice cold, the wind biting into the flesh. The figure scurried over to the edge of the house and looked around. Everything was asleep. The ground even seemed to pulse with its slumber. Later, he realized it was merely his beating heart.

The figure walked a few hundred yards away from the house towards a small cliff embankment. There he stood and gazed out on the valley below. The sight was glorious!

All the trees swayed in unison with one another, a huge orchestra playing a symphony. And he, he was their director. He marveled at the beauty of the trees crashing on top one another as the breeze commanded them. Branches bent, leaves blew away and the wind continued to howl. The figure turned to look back the way he had come but it all seemed so much further away now than a few moments ago. He seemed to be falling, but yet was still standing. The ground felt moist beneath his feet, but no rain had fallen. Amongst the chaos he saw a light down in the distance. At first he thought he was seeing things but the light sparked again, then again, each time nearing. The figure stared awestruck at its beauty, captivated that such a thing could exist.

Minutes passed and he remained unmoved from his gaze. Several more had passed and he hadn't even noticed the light was within touching distance from his face. Soon the light, clear as day yet dark as night, drifted around his body and caressed his shoulders with its fingers. The glow was warm and had a chill about it, almost deathly. Up ahead the clouds shifted and grew in magnitude. Great storm clouds formed and billowed atop each other, each trying to trample the other to the top. Thunder rolled and echoed through the valley floor. A soft drizzle began to sleet itself down from the heavens wetting the forest earth. The figure stood there still, untouched by the rain. With no warning the light began to fade away, lingering just enough to tempt the figure to follow. He did so willingly. Down the slopes he followed. Into thicket and mush he sloshed. Within minutes he was swallowed whole by the enormity of the forest, lost to the world outside. The figure parted another branch from his face and came into an open cavity in the brush. A stream made homage here, a refuge amongst the debris of the wood. Something was different about this riverbed. It seemed to sway from side to side unlike the natural one-way flow, seemingly to gain strength and life each time a wave crashed into another.

Such strange behavior for a river.

The earth, it too had a strangeness about it. It seemed to tug at you, dragging you closer. But closer to what? There it was. All at once, the voice so sweet and melodious came and caressed his ears. So soft and welcoming, none could deny its calling. Fear seemed to grip the figure but a strange glow evaporated from the water which made him feel curious.

"Come…"

The figure looked around startled and confused. The voice spoke, a woman? The figure couldn't see where the voice was coming from. "Come Raifen. I want to show you something." As if in hypnosis, he followed. Raifen stepped wearily into the water, afraid it to have hidden sinkholes that would catch him, or the rushing water to take him away. To his surprise, neither happened and not only that, Raifen seemed to float along the water, almost as if it weren't water at all but some other substance.

Raifen soon reached the other side and found the ground to be softer, more bouncy than normal earth. Raifen felt like a rabbit or some sort of small creature hopping around. He almost smirked but realized—the animals? Where were the animals? All around the figure were trees, trees and trees. He could see no sign of a living creature. Unease crept its way into his soul. The place appeared abandoned and empty. But still there was a chill in his breath that told him to not believe the unseen. There was some evil magic about, he could feel it. If he wasn't careful, it would have him in chains.

"Where am I?" asked Raifen.

As if the ghostly voice heard his thoughts, she spoke, foretelling of the mysteriousness of the place. "You are in a place no longer here nor there. No longer past, nor present. A place where time does not exist."

Her words chilled Raifen to the bones. He felt weak. He seemed to be having trouble standing. The place was called Amaranth as the voice later told, meaning eternally beautiful, unfading, and everlasting. *Ironic, as the place was not to exist.*

Raifen walked further and came to a narrow levee leading to an open space some thirty feet below, where the voice seemed to have vanished to and now was commencing speech. A faint blue light was transforming, devouring itself then coming back.

Raifen had almost climbed down the embankment completely and made his way through some more trees. There was barely enough footing for Raifen on the cliff so he had to walk slow and sort of wind around it in a diagonal, in the meantime trying not to fall. Many sharp and dangerous boulders and rocks sat at the bottom, waiting for him to slip so they could catch him. The effort to not fall down took the wind out of Raifen and he leaned over a small rock nearby to catch him breath.

The voice suddenly spoke again, but this time it wasn't as peaceful. It seemed urgent, telling him to hurry, to come quickly. It said they didn't have much time. Raifen pressed on even though he didn't understand. He moved anxiously, the trees catching his face and smacking him harder each time he passed. Once he reached the bottom where the voice was calling, the lights flickered and suddenly went out. Raifen paused in his progression, standing still for what seemed like an eternity. He was trapped in a cocoon of darkness. It was almost as if it were suffocating him, but at the same time, lifting him.

Raifen wondered if these were imaginations or real. All these passed away as suddenly as they came when the light flashed right in front of his face. He flinched at the sudden outburst of light and squinted his eyes shut immediately, gradually peering out from under cracked lids. In the beginning the light was merely a spark but soon began to pulse like a heart beat, booming and exploding into many different colors: deep blue, blood red, turquoise, and heavenly green. It was beautiful and breathtaking, dangerously breathtaking. Raifen stood paralyzed by the beauty, dumbfounded and in wonder of the colors which were now fluttering all around him, grasping him and holding him still. From amongst the colors arose a face, shaded by its bluish hair that sheltered it. She then peered up at him with two silhouette eyes of reds, blues, and greens, with a little hint of yellow in them. The same color as his. She smiled at him and he at her. He couldn't help it, she was so magnificent! She was so beautiful, so captivating, that she made the heavens seem mere mystified illusions.

"Hello, Raifen," she spoke. "I have been waiting for you. The time has come for you to finally know." Raifen didn't have a clue what she meant by finally being able to know so he asked her.

"Know what?"

"Why, the truth," she answered.

"Who are you and why did you ask me to follow?"

"Oh dear, my oh my, that old hag. I can't believe he let him grow up without knowing his true heritage and where he's come from. Oh, when I get my hands on that no good excuse for an uncle…" Raifen couldn't help, but noticed she was now talking to herself, this thing, her temper seeming to rise. Raifen was busy trying to figure out what was happening to notice that the light which he had been following, the one that glowed and radiated all around her body, now changed. It no longer was the nice white light that had led him through the trees or darkness to this place. No, it now hovered on the brink of bright red, masking and covering her entire body in a cocoon of scarlet mist. Raifen never noticed this until later for he was too preoccupied with the thoughts of who this woman might actually be. She gave him a strange feeling inside, as if he knew her. Yet, he knew he had never met her before in his life. But still, the uneasiness bestowed itself inside him, boiling. Raifen couldn't handle not knowing, "Excuse me," he said, "what's your name and what about this uncle you speak of?"

The woman snapped back as if realizing where she was for the first time and who she was with, coming back to her senses. Just then, Raifen finally took into account what she had become. No longer the beautiful thing he had first imagined. Instead, she was dark looking, almost evil-like in color and presence. She herself did not change though as he had noticed but rather the air and light around her did, into a red curtain of darkness. But as she came back from her ill-tempered masquerade, she returned to her lovely, almost blinding beauty. It suited her, he thought.

"Oh sorry dear. I was caught up with myself. I apologize" she said rather empathetically.

Obviously, thought Raifen. The woman glared at him momentarily. Raifen saw this and stepped back, alert with this new wave of surprise.

"Now for your questions. The first one shall be answered first. Or if you would like I could start with the second or the third one first. Or start with the third then the second and then the first. Or the second, then the third, then the first. Or—"

"No. Don't worry about the order. Just answer the questions and more I might have," said Raifen hurriedly.

"Why of course my dear, if that's what you prefer, then I shall abide by your wishes."

"Doesn't seem I have any other choice, now do I?

She seemed to smile at him.

"Now, let's see. My name is Cossett. And as for—"

"Excuse me miss. Did you say your name was Cossett?" he asked.

"Why yes, yes I did." A wry and knowing smile crossed her perfect face. Raifen froze. *Could this be he kept asking himself.*

"Yes," she said.

She's gone, thought Raifen.

"No," the woman said.

A deep sadness harvested itself inside Raifen. The news had been too much. It couldn't be. It just couldn't. He wouldn't allow his mind to believe it. *His mother's name was none other than Cossett. Could this be his mother* he thought? *Or just a woman with the same name?* No, it couldn't possibly be his mother, she was dead. *Right? How could it be her?* Raifen still wasn't sure. He couldn't allow himself to think that it was really his mother. After all these years without her, never even seeing her face, he just couldn't accept it. Though deep down inside his gut he longed for it to be the truth. Oh, how long he had wished he could have seen his mother. To touch her and to be held by her firm and loving hands. To cry on her shoulder when he was hurting or upset. To have a companion to talk too. And now he might be getting his wish. Raifen silently prayed to himself. Please. Please. Please let it be true. Please.

Cossett, the ghostly woman, seemed to have heard his thoughts for she gently said, "Yes dear, I am. You a child, and I a young woman, at the time of departure. Now I am only grieved to say it shall be the next soon." She reached out and took her son in her hands. She wrapped her arms around him and soothed him like she would a small child. Raifen did not care. He wrapped his arms around her too. Squeezing and absorbing her with his body. She smelled so sweet. She felt so smooth. She was so perfect. Just as he had imagined she would.

"You're a blessing to me my son. Don't ever forget that. You have something extraordinary inside of you. Something very special, waiting to be released and show you the way,

MATTHEW THRUSH

your path that you must take, the long, twisted, and dangerous road that lays before you now."

"But…m-mother how c-can it be?" Raifen asked. His hands were shaking. An anxious smile crossed her face. She replied with much enthusiastic cheer, "I am the guardian of this place. We spirits call it Amaranth. When I died bringing you into the world, you still were capable of using your powers even if you didn't consciously know it. You willed me to not leave you forever, to remain forever close to you. And so, that is why I am here, a little way from the old farm. I have been watching you for some time now, but never was the time until now to talk to you. I sure wish your uncle would have told you a little about who you really are." Raifen seemed to be thinking of something in his past. His faced filled with recognition of something forgotten.

"Uncle Seraph did tell me a little. He said that you were killed giving birth, and that dad left. He said it wouldn't be a good idea to tell me in great detail about what had been happening here of late, since I was only a child then. I did catch some things that I bet he hoped I wouldn't hear and notice."

Raifen smiled with a wry knowing smile of mischief.

"The clouds as I noticed always seemed to be darker. I never knew quite why it was. I overheard Uncle Seraph talking to some of the town folk when he went to get some more barley and flour about this same occurrence. I was in the wagon. Uncle Seraph had told me to stay put and I had done so obediently at least for a little while, but I couldn't resist the temptation to get out and wander around a little. I was talking with the other children, the normal fantasy stuff where you imagine you are some powerful war lord fighting dragons and what not, when I heard it."

Raifen paused in his retelling of what he knew about himself. He seemed to have dozed off into another world, thinking of the future and how he would like to be, remembering the day when he heard the acrid voice, so venomous and foul. The voice seemed to be talking as if it were giving orders. *Orders to whom?* Raifen did not know. He just listened. Raifen didn't know what it was at the time, but he had a feeling about this voice, a feeling of determination to vanquish it to Dalek, a place where demons are imprisoned, opposite of where the gods reside—a hell. The voice only lasted briefly but for those few seconds Raifen had experienced something he had never felt before … the desire of revenge.

"Raifen, what is it dear?" his concerned mother asked. She could see the turmoil and anguish contorting his face as he fought against some unseen foe.

"I was just reliving a memory of mine when I was young. Nothing really," Raifen said.

"What did you hear, dear? You said you got out of the wagon, were with the other children, and that's when you said you heard it. What was it that you heard?" asked Cossett, waiting patiently for the reply.

Again the same blank stare of remembrance shadowed itself upon Raifen's brow. He seemed to not be in his own world, alone, and in the middle of nowhere, with no life to be seen. Raifen heard a voice, yet this one was different from the bitter one. He heard a comforting sound, someone calling his name. The world of Raifen's memory started to fade away, and became blurry. A new place began to come into focus, with an older short stubby man with a look of worry upon his face, looking down at him.

"Raifen, are you okay?"

"Yes. I'm fine. Just had a bad dream is all," answered Raifen, but inside he knew it was something much more than that. He rubbed his head, swiping the sweat away from its rim.

Seraph looked a bit distraught and worried for his nephew, but he kept his thoughts to himself for the moment. It had been strange from the beginning of the story his Raifen had been telling him some hours ago, but he had become tired in the telling and went to bed. Hours had gone by and he still remained asleep. Seraph was in the living room when he had first heard the moans before they became something more. Raifen's hair looked as if it had gone through a brush fire and now flared in all directions as he sat on the edge of his bed. Just a few moments ago as Seraph was rethinking, Raifen was thrashing around in his sheets, screaming a name.

Beshaahoo.

Seraph's hands shook violently. He seemed to hardly be able to contain himself. He knew what this word meant and the importance of his nephew saying it. He would try to make sure he didn't say why it bothered him so too soon. Things should not be urged on too quickly. Especially one of this magnitude. His fear that was raging deep within his heart cascaded down through his veins and up his arms, legs, fingers, toes, and face. His whole body went into spasm with the tension that was being spent and distributed.

When Raifen had come to, he was horrified at first glance at his uncle. Pale with fright and a deluge of perspiration streaming down his face, horror spoke through his eyes. Twisted and tongue-tied, Seraph couldn't voice his accusations at first. After coming to, Raifen seemed to notice this on his Uncle's face too, for he jumped back in shock. A few seconds passed and not a word was said. Then slowly, as if unsure of himself, Raifen dared to ask the question.

"What is it, U-u-ncle?" motioned Raifen with his eyes, pleading for his uncle's response.

"You were screaming in your sleep," began Seraph, "tossing and turning as if in a hurricane."

Raifen seemed to relax more by this account.

"But, that's not all that you were doing. You were yelling a name. That name was Beshaahooo."

I know *you* know.

Why was his nephew speaking these words? I thought only the ones who have *seen* the Bringer of Death voice them? Is there more to this than meets the eye? The thoughts went unnoticed and unaccounted for as they flew within Seraph's head. Only he knew the enormity of this little event. One, he must be careful to not allow to get ahead of him. A serious awakening was in effect and he must be sure to guide it the way it should go. Seraph would make sure he looked into it. A close eye would be kept on his nephew from now on, anything else would be foolish. Apparently, it had begun.

Seraph paused and took a breath. Seraph's eyes shined down on Raifen as he continued voicing his fears.

"That's not the thing that frightened me most. Though it holds a strong meaning."

Raifen looked back up at his uncle, wondering what could be worse.

"It was the fact that you had a smile on your face when saying it," Seraph said, his heart skipped a beat as he thought about what this could mean.

Smiling. Smiling? *Is there some evil in work here? Has Raifen been contacted by the Bringer of Death personally? Should I be concerned? I should let the Elders know of this, but how will I get there without alerting Raifen?* He must not know of this yet. If he knew, it could be disastrous.

Raifen was stunned. Why would this bother his uncle so much; it was just a dream after all, wasn't it?

"Why would that bother you so?" asked Raifen, voicing his thoughts. Seraph sighed and gestured for Raifen to sit. Seraph had decided he should tell Raifen a little about his destiny. *A little wouldn't hurt, would it?* He would make sure he didn't say too much. He must let Raifen remain in ignorance. Only there was he truly safe. So Seraph thought.

"I guess it is time I told you something about the ages." Seraph clenched his fingers together in a tight knot before beginning. He knew what he would say next would have a tremendous effect on the outcome of his nephew. He meant to make sure it stayed a good one.

"A long time ago when the sky was filled with darkness, much as it is now, the land was overflowing with Talions. This period of time was known as the time of the Bringer of Death. It was a time of pain and a time of no hope. A time of fear and terror. A time when no one dared to leave their houses, though remaining in your house would not aid you or provide refuge. You were unsafe. People were being tortured and burned right in front of their families. The Fangoers would come and ravage the young women viciously, and eat the newborns in front of their terrified mothers, while the Talions came and destroyed town after town. The whole world was in chaos. Families would try to flee to other lands, unsuccessfully, for the enemy followed." Raifen's face was white and his eyes glowed a fiery red. It was obvious his temper was beginning to fume from this news of such vileness.

"This wasn't the worst of all things." continued Seraph. "The Bringer of Death had some special creatures which he sent out to gather the remaining *soon to be dead* humans. He called them the Axions. They were known to come and help themselves to the cattle and little children for their little snack on the way back from doing the Bringer of Death's bidding. These were awful things. They smelled of dead carcasses and wore forsaken cloaks of the dead. They were dreadful to look upon. Spirit like, our forefathers who betrayed their people and joined with the Bringer of Death, summoned directly from Dalek itself to rein havoc on the world. No one knows quite why they abandoned their kind, but sometimes when the night is asleep and the wind is snoring, you can hear them screaming and crying, begging for forgiveness. The tales say of their regretting ever having joined Vlandrax Xen, but they still remain in Dalek guarded by Huruak, the monstrosity of death. Until called upon, they cannot leave. That's why they were of the greatest disasters when set loose, because of their eternal imprisonment. For when out, they took advantage of their freedom and brought suffering to all they came across. They wanted others to feel as much pain and horror as they did. No one could escape them. They can see through walls and smell the fresh flesh upon others backs. It seemed to many that all hope was lost, but then *they* came."

"Whose *they* Uncle?" asked Raifen.

He seemed to be drawn to this conversation with his Uncle, especially concerning the ones he called "*they*." He had a feeling in his heart as if he knew them already. As if he belonged and was being spoken to in his heart by *them*.

"*They* are called the Nazracs, my son," replied Seraph. "They came from the south. No one knew quite sure where or who they were and came from, but all we cared was that they came to help us. And help us they did. The Nazracs had some different approaches to fending off the Bringer of Death, the ways only known by their people. And the Bringer of Death was called something different by them—they called him by the name of Raifen."

Raifen jolted. A stunned look branched his face.

"Why Uncle, that's my name," shuddered Raifen.

"Yes, I know. That's why I kept the truth from you for so long. I was afraid if I told you the truth that you would leave. I'm sorry I never told you before." His uncle drooped his head to his chest out of shame.

"If my name is Raifen and that's the name given of the Bringer of Death, then why don't the people in town fear me?" asked Raifen, more curious than frightened at the time being.

Seraph frowned, "Because I told everyone else that your name was Genesis."

"Genesis? Why did you say my name was Genesis, Uncle?" returned Raifen.

"Remember how I said that the Nazracs had their own ways of things, and they called the Bringer of Death, *Vlandrax Xen*?" began Seraph

"Yes," replies Raifen.

"His full name was Raifen Vlandrax Xen, the Bringer of Death."

Raifen just stared in bewilderment and shock.

"Raifen thought his first name was weak and therefore went by his middle and last name accordingly. He felt they bestowed power and command." Seraph paused to think to make sure he got his thoughts correct.

"Well, while they were here, they predicted a prophecy. That prophecy was that a new hope would come and fight off the Bringer of Death. He would be known as Raifen Vlandrax Genesis. The Bringer of Hope. They also said that this boy's parents would be born in the upcoming years. They said that one would be born to them by the name of Raifen Genesis, the new light. This new Raifen that they predicted was to be born some hundred years later for his parents were not to be born yet, but would be soon. I was only twelve at the time. Your father's parents and mine heard of the prophecy, for the prophecy was told to the Genesis' and they were friends with the Dovetails, your mother's parents. Only a few knew of this prophecy. So whenever someone would have a child we were told to check for certain signs of the prophesied birth. A small white patch would glow between the baby's eyes, with a mist flowing down to their heart, were a few of them. None were born according to their description for years. The towns' people never knew quite why we were so eager to see their new born babes, but only that we were told to. We said nothing else about the prophecy.

"Only my family, few others, and I knew of its existence. But then, many years later we finally found it, or them, as we should say. One day, while we were doing our normal chores and assignments of the day, a messenger came running from town into my father's room. I could not hear completely what was being said but I could tell my father was excited. Shortly after, both my father and I, along with the messenger, left the house. My father had told me that something exciting was happening. At first I was to stay, but I pleaded with him to let me join and he, being in such high spirits, soon obliged. Down the road we went. Fast too, as I remember. My father was urging the horses on as if he were running away from some wild beast. We soon came into town. All was normal except for one small house. Inside there came rushing forth a great commotion.

"My father leapt off the wagon and ran into the house. I followed soon after. I did not wish to miss anything. My eyes were peeled and I watched closely for what was taking place. As I entered I soon realized that my hopes were to be dwindled. In one of the rooms, lying side by side, were my mother and another woman. I had known something was wrong with my mother before, weeks and months before, when her stomach began to get abnormally large. I had never seen this happen before and was worried for her.

My father had told me not to worry, and so, I didn't. My mother had been away from the house for a few weeks now. My father said it was for her own benefit that she remains in the town. He had said that the baby was due any day now. *Baby?* I had thought to myself. *What's a baby?* And so, I stood there by the door that led to where my mother now lay, screaming. I began to cry and plead with my father that she was hurting and that something was terribly wrong, but he had just smiled and said, "It is soon."

"*Soon? What's soon?* She's in pain and you're just going to stand here and let her take it? Are you mad? Why are you smiling? I had many thoughts racing through my mind but they halted when I heard another yelp of some other woman. I peered through my father's and the other peoples' arms and saw who was crying also. It was the other woman I had seen lying next to my mother on a different opposing bed. Apparently, she too was going through the same pain and turmoil that my mother was going through. And to add to my astonishment, the man standing next to her was her husband. This was not what shocked me, but the fact that he was smiling too, just as my father was. *Strange.* Strange things were happening and I did not understand their depth.

"I guess I was too young at the time to know the truth of what was happening. Both my mother and the other woman were pregnant, and they were in labor. And soon, they would have a baby. One each, as usual standards asked. But sometimes, as I noticed later on as the years went by, some people had more than one baby at a time. It was considered a great miracle for this to take place. I still did not

MATTHEW THRUSH

understand these people. And what were these little half-lings coming out of these women? Were they some kind of demon-possessed peoples? These people of the town somehow got a hold of my mother, too. I would put a stop to this one way or the next. As I went to enter the room, something weird happened. As I slid through the legs of my father and another man, my eyes fell on my mother. And what I saw then would change my life forever. Out of her private part, something was exiting. Indeed these people are possessed, and now they have my mother. Though I was horrified at the reality of what was taking place, I could not but help being a little curious at the same time. I watched, rather awkwardly as the *thing* came out of my mother. I call it a thing for I knew not what else to classify it as. And oddly, this *thing* resembled a human. In fact, it looked a lot like my father with a few dashes of my mother here and there. I remember tilting my head in wonder as this *thing* of new life sprouted from my mother's body. I knew not the magnitude of the situation. I was still far too young.

"Someone, the one who was tending to my mother as this *thing* came from her, was now holding it in his hands. A damp cloth lay in his hands and he gently wiped at the *thing's* face and body. Also, as I noticed, he had some kind of tool in his pocket. He later used this weapon to cut some weird looking intestine from the *thing's* body. All the while the *thing* in his hands was crying or screaming, whichever one fits the definition best when nothing can be heard. As if my ear drums didn't already have enough to deal with, another little creature came from the other woman's private place as well. Just as my mother had done, this woman too gave life to a demon. Oddly, this one too looked like the one standing near. *Strange. Whatever kind of madness this was, it was strange indeed.* As my eardrums later began to take on their normal feeling and volume, the two women, my mother and this other lady, both lay there on the beds, holding their little screaming *things*. Let them, I thought. They'll soon realize what they've done when they finally come to and notice they have demons in their hands, sprouted from their own bodies. I could not take it any-more so I left the room. I went outside and sat down next to the dirt road on the wagon. A soft breeze ruffled my hair. I felt a few moments later a pair of strong hands clenching my shoulders. I turned in surprise and relaxed when I saw my father standing over me.

'Your mother has had a little baby girl,' he had said to me. 'Do you want to know what her name is?' he had asked. I had shrugged. 'Her name is Cossett. Our little Cossett and your baby sister.' I had sneered at him. I didn't ask for a baby sister, I had thought. Why give it to me? Give it to someone else who wants one. I sure don't. My father qui-etly sat there next to me for a while and then left me and went back into the house. I remained there until late in the night. My father finally came back out and seemed pleased with how things were progressing and he was glowing with pride. He got back in the wagon and pulled on the reins of the horses. He looked down at me, me and my poor pathetic self, sitting on the road. He just smiled.

'Ready boy?' he asked. 'We're going home.' I stood up, rather slowly, and climbed up into the wagon. My father put his arm around me and we started off. On the way home he

MATTHEW THRUSH

talked a lot. Much of things I didn't much care about and didn't even understand. I learned that the other woman had had her baby as well and that his name was Anathema. I brushed these words aside, but would later realize just how important they were. Now I can tell you without feeling guilty or ashamed, I know now that what my feelings were at the time were wrong. But that can be expected from a twelve-year-old. And as the Nazracs had prophesied, the Genesis' son was to be called Anathema and the Dovetails' daughter to be named Cossett. And it was done so. The prophecy has lived on all these years, through your father's families and mine. The signs were evident in both children and concurred our thoughts and hopes. We have tried to keep it as much of a secret as we could. We did not want to be getting too much attention drawn to ourselves. Not to mention awaken the Bringer of Death's attention to us, since he had retreated and gone into hiding some ten years after the Nazracs came. As far as we know, the Bringer of Death returned to his fortress in Uzunia. The Nazracs stayed for a short time afterwards and left only after they told your father's parents the prophecy to come."

Seraph stopped and looked at his nephew straight in the eyes, all seriousness endowed.

"So Raifen, do you see you are the importance of this world? The thing this world has been waiting for. Your birth has been foretold for years and now, here you are. The son of Anathema and Cossett Genesis, just as it is written in the prophecies."

While Seraph paused to let the information sink in, Raifen was trying to make sense of everything his uncle had just told him, putting this new meaning now so suddenly in his life. He couldn't find the missing pieces and therefore was bound to ask for some guidance of his uncle.

"Uncle, what does this necessarily mean to me?" asked Raifen trying to connect the missing puzzle pieces of his life and fate. "What does this mean I am supposed to do?"

A worried and yet still tender smile seemed to come upon his uncle's face.

"You are the Bringer of Hope. Nothing is supposed to be easy and no one has all the answers, especially me."

Seraph allowed a chuckle to escape his lips.

"I know a few things to get you started, but you will have to journey to Petipala to learn the ways of power to their full extent. I only know how you can use your powers and what happens. You know that birthmark on your chest by your heart?" asked Seraph.

"Yes," replied Raifen.

He felt the place where the birthmark was with his fingertips, rubbing the outline of the forest, the trees and sky that it appears as. Ever since he could remember, he had always had it.

"Well," started Seraph, "when you use your power, it glows bright reddish-purple. It's like a warning to you and anyone else that sees it that you have the power. It's the key to unlocking your true gifts and showing you the way. I'm not totally sure how you use it, but the Nazracs left a hint to achieving it." He left the room and came back shortly with an old, crippled up piece of parchment. He undid the red string tied around it and unfolded it to its full length. Some pieces of the paper were missing and Seraph had to read slowly and squint at the lettering to be able to read all that was on its surface.

He read:

> with you always big or small,
> in a child while he crawls,
> is when sprung,
> is when young,
> is everywhere,
> is when he is scared,
> with you when you leave,
> with you when you can't see,
> there when old,
> there when not so bold,
> look in the heart and let it happen,
> you decide you are captain,
> see it as it is,
> it is truth, it is his …

"It ended there but there were bits and pieces of it missing. They said that the rest would have to be found by the one who is destined for great things. A little riddle for you to figure out and I guess when you find your way, you will be able to use it. Or by what I believe, could use it all along. I'm sorry I couldn't help you much, I was never one for riddles or special talents."

The last words of his uncle were lost to Raifen. He was already thinking about what it all meant and what he was supposed to do if in fact this riddle was meant for him. And if it was meant for him, how was he going to be able to break the code and understand its meanings.

"Where is this place the Nazracs call home?" asked Raifen all at once.

"Oh, somewhere south I suppose. No one knows really where they came from, just by what the stories say."

"Is there anyone that knows the old stories?" asked Raifen, hopeful.

His uncle didn't answer at first, but then his face lit up with what appeared as a new enlightenment.

"I know of a storyteller." He held his finger to his chin in concentration and thought.

"Can he help us?" asked Raifen.

"I think he might."

A pleased Raifen smiled.

"Where is this storyteller?" asked Raifen eagerly.

"Blasa. I think. I can't be sure," answered Seraph.

"Well, what are we waiting for then? Let's go," an impatient Raifen urged. And he stood up, acting as if he was going to walk out the front door right then and there.

"What do you mean let's go?" frowned Seraph.

Raifen smirked, "Of course Uncle, you don't have to come along if you don't feel fit enough to." Raifen was purposely prodding his uncle's macho ego to his assistance. Shame on himself, he thought, but he needed his uncle's help to find this place. Apparently, it had worked.

"I am more fit than you are at wandering aimlessly through the countryside," defensive Seraph snapped.

Raifen laughed, grinning all the more flamboyantly.

"Of course you are, Uncle. Why else would I want you to come along if not for keeping me from going astray?"

Seraph seemed to take that last compliment well, as

it visibly bolstered his self-confidence. Seraph pondered the task for a second then stood proud and straight and continued.

"We can't go wandering through the wilderness without supplies. We'll leave in a few days from now. Until then, we should probably tend to the animals and gather food and clothing for the journey." Seraph's voice changed to one of seriousness.

"Raifen if you would, please finish your chores and we'll talk some more tonight."

"Yes uncle, I will do that," replied Raifen, a little saddened by this change in timeline. But he would obey. Besides, he had more than enough on his mind to keep him occupied while finishing his chores.

DANGER IN THE NIGHT

That night the wind blew harder than usual, it seemed to almost rip the roots of these age-old trees fresh out of the fertile soil. Wild coyote and moose wails trailed through the wind, along with a many other things. A strong breeze blew in from the southeastern border, causing Raifen to struggle more against Mother Nature and her ally, the gale wind from the east, making it difficult gathering the sheep. The chickens kept getting excited and hooting every time a crashing thunderbolt would sound, which did not aid in making things easier. Not to mention his dog Bestrow, a strong Great Dane with a hint of beagle and more like a miniature bear, kept barking at the nothingness that had surrounded him. That only added to the chickens' wild frenzied onslaught. A light drizzle of silk rain drops began falling down. The land was not yet in complete darkness, for the sun had not vanished its light from the world just yet. Raifen hurried to gather all the animals together, but there was always that one sheep that would always get itself lost. *Babylon.* She was not nearly four months old, and struggled to walk with three normal-sized legs and one gimp one. Raifen always felt pity for this lamb. Not just because she looked so weak and useless, but also because he saw the way the other sheep treated her. He saw something inside her that he wished he had himself. Her spirit was so free-minded, something Raifen truly wished he had. No matter how much the other sheep bullied her around, she still seemed to keep a smile on her

MATTHEW THRUSH

face. Always running about happily as if she had not a care in the world.

"She lost herself again Uncle," Raifen called to his uncle.

"Don't be long now you hear? Raifen, a storm is a-brewin' and I don't want you getting caught up in it," yelled Seraph, concerned for his nephew's safety.

"Don't worry Uncle, I can take care of myself. I won't be gone for long." And he was gone before Seraph could say another word.

Raifen headed straight for the old oak tree by the riverbed. Babylon normally was to be found there, curled up under a little cliff next to a field of multi-colored flowers. Raifen made his way hurriedly, for the rain was coming more violently now. Raifen could hardly see through the pouring rain and the thicket of trees and light underbrush. Raifen stopped suddenly, he heard something up ahead. It didn't sound like the young innocent lamb he knew. There was a tearing and scratching sound on rock just ahead through the thicket. An animal moaned. Raifen slowly and carefully made his way closer, trying not to make a sound.

How stupid, Raifen thought to himself, I can't be heard in this deafening noise. But nonetheless, he continued cautiously as he made his way to the mountainside just up ahead. Nearly five feet ahead, he heard it again, a loud screeching cry, drawing tears to his eyes. An animal was in danger, or hurt, or both, begging for assistance of any kind. Raifen had to help. He busted through the trees with only a few strides and saw then what was causing all the commotion. A giant god-like bear on four legs, covered in fur, was not fifteen feet away. The crying animal was completely wound up with excitement. It was Babylon trapped between a one-square-foot area, with the overpowering bear clawing his way through, desperately trying to free the lamb of its temporary refuge. Raifen didn't have much time to gather up a plan. He had to hurry or the life of his favorite lamb would be lost. He reached up over his shoulder where his bow normally hung, but it wasn't there. He cursed silently for not bringing it. He looked around his surroundings for something to use as a temporary weapon. He spotted a medium-sized stick, some three inches around and about three feet long, though somewhat crooked, not more than a foot or two away. He made for it. The bear must have heard him and it turned around.

Raifen froze, standing stock-still, making eye contact with the beast. A fiery hatred seemed to rage within the bear's eyes as they glowed bright red with blood lust, as if it were displeased by the unexpected disturbance. Fear filled Raifen's head, but only for a few seconds. This was strange given his current situation and the odds against him. A weird uneasy feeling crept up on Raifen. He heard, no, *felt* something like a voice speaking to him in his head.

You can do this.

Confidence swelled up inside Raifen. He turned to face the bear. I can do this, you can do this, it won't beat me, it can't beat me. These words were running around inside Raifen's head as he heard himself talking to himself. Yet, it wasn't actually him talking, *was it?*

"I won't let you," was Raifen's last thought when the bear burst towards him with its inflamed anger having boiled

over and now steaming its insides and him meeting it head on. As Raifen stood starring at the bear, the purple-red mist began to swirl around his hands. Soon, they were not hands at all, but merely a source of power. Soon the bear would get a taste of what real anger felt like, real strength.

SURVIVAL

He stumbled along, weakly. Tired to the point of dropping, he finally did so. He lay just outside the small cave-like structure that constituted the small lamb's asylum. Catching his breath, heaving with each intake, he slipped slowly out from under the now dead body on the ground. The creature's form cast against the deadening earth, adding to its richness, the body already beginning to decompose. The fight between human and animal did not last long at all. It seemed the war was over before it ever started. The bear had had no chance. Though you would have thought it the other way around.

As soon as Raifen touched the beast, hands on fire with red and purple flames, it withered up and died at his feet, melting into a pile of dried flesh. Raifen had wrestled the bear to the ground and willed for the bear to die. *Willed it. How strange. How tributary.* A few scratches and mud stains were all Raifen had suffered. Each of which was the cause of worming his way out from underneath the heap of dead meat, which was the bear, or what was left of it that was. The lamb, sensing there was still danger near, stayed huddled in the far end of the cave-like den. Raifen crouched, reached in, and grabbed the frightened Babylon.

"It's okay, now, you're safe my little friend," spoke Raifen, encouraging the lamb. Raifen gently stroked the lamb on the head and gave it a little kiss on the nose. Looking into Babylon's innocent eyes filled Raifen with a new wave of sympathy for the young adolescent lamb.

"Let's go home, young one," comforted Raifen. The little, clearly weakened, lamb struggled to get onto its feet. Raifen, almost by instinct, picked her up in his arms and made way for the farm. But he knew if he did so, she would not grow to be as strong as she could be. He would always be there to help her, but she must first attempt to do it on her own.

MINDLESS TASKS

The fire in the living room burned brighter than ever after being fueled with more dry-rotted wood by Seraph. Seraph was sitting on a rocking chair holding a book in his hands, but unable to read its words, wondering if Raifen was all right. He also thought about the journey the next day. He had been sitting there for a few hours now and still Raifen hadn't returned. Seraph decided he needed to do something, to move around, instead of sitting there reading, which of course he hadn't even accomplished. Seraph picked up a broom and began to twirl the stick in his hand. He walked around the house brushing the dirt into a small pile in the center of the main room. He continued to do so for a few minutes, but every time thunder rang in the distance, which seemed to be striking within his mind, he fluttered and the broom shot the dirt from the pile into far off corners of the room. And each time, he would go and sweep it back to the center pile and each time he would reach it, another bolt would sound, as if kissing the roof of the house, and he would send the pile of dirt skidding across the floor again. After about the third time, he cursed aloud and stopped sweeping. It was a mindless task anyway. He just had to keep himself occupied with something or he would go insane with worry. It was too late for him though, his worst fears began to rumble and grow, multiplying on themselves tenfold as he continued to voice his concerns within his mind. A sense of worry seeped through his thoughts and his breaths even came in shallow gasps at times. When he thought he heard some-thing, but it turned out that it was just the wind screeching against the sides of the house, he began to become more upset. Seraph had given up on trying to listen for Raifen's return, it proved too pointless. Each second there would come another sound, and each time it would be to no array. It did not surprise him one bit when he heard the gate shut and some stumbling footsteps and a sound as if someone were carrying a load extra in their hands coming up the front porch. He did not even bother with this sound. Not even when the door knob seemed to twitch. But soon, as if he were jolted, Seraph jumped up off the rocker as if he were a bird taking flight and peered anxiously at the front door. There had been something different about this last noise, something strange. As if there weren't really a noise coming but some kind of silent force. It did surprise him, though, when his nephew opened the door.

WISDOM GAINED

O nce getting home from his little quest for Babylon, Raifen made sure the rest of the sheep and animals were safe and secure from the downpour. After checking the gate to be firmly shut and latched, he made his way to the house. The porch light was shining carelessly through the glimmering thunder. There was a smell of fried chicken floating through the air, with an extra scent of rice and corn for a side dish every now and then catching Raifen in the nose and making his eyes water with delight.

Seraph must be cooking, drenched Raifen said to himself.

"Smells like chicken and garlic sauce melted into the belly of the bird. You like chicken don't you, Babylon?" asked Raifen in a joyful manner. The lamb looked up at him as if replying, yes. Raifen knew the lamb didn't know what he was talking about. Sheep don't eat chicken, and in turn chicken don't eat sheep. The system is a solid one.

Raifen gently opened the door, trying not to disturb his uncle if he were reading or something. Right as Raifen stepped one foot in the door, his uncle nearly strangled him with his searching hands. His uncle seemed to be looking for any signs of a wound and he got more than that.

"What happened to you, Raifen, I was worried something terrible happened to you? I thought you had fallen in a ditch or gotten stuck in the storm. What is all this blood all over your cloak? Have you been hurt? Anything broken?" asked Seraph, more worried than he was.

"No, I'm fine uncle, just fought with a deadly bear is all," said Raifen, smirking at his uncle.

"A bear?" Seraph asked and yelled simultaneously. "But—how?"

"I'm not really sure myself uncle, just one second I was running at him and him at me, and the next second I know it was lying dead next to me. I remember feeling something inside me when I first attacked it. It was like I was able to control what happened. I was telling myself that I could do this and it couldn't stop me," replied Raifen, remembering back on the bear attack.

"And it didn't. I killed it with my own hands, without a weapon cause I left my knife and bow here when I went out. My chest hurt, too, Uncle. I had this stinging pain that seemed to come from inside of me. I felt the bones of the bear's back break in my hands and its heart when it stopped beating. It was weird. Something I've never felt before."

A calmer Seraph looked his nephew in the eyes, he seemed to have seen something else for a second then it must have disappeared for his face muscles contracted back to normal.

"It seems to me Raifen, that you have started to understand how to use your gift. You say you felt it did you? Strange. Strange indeed. We'll have to wait until we talk to the *Healer* in Petipala to hear what he thinks. For now there is nothing we can do but be thankful that the circumstances weren't worse. Things could be much more worse off for us at the moment," reasoned Seraph.

He walked over and put his hand on Raifen's shoulder as a father would do when being grateful that nothing happened to his son when everything could have been so much different.

"I'm just glad you're safe now," a fatherly Seraph says. "You get some sleep now, we have a big day ahead of us tomorrow."

"Alright Uncle, I will. Good night, Uncle Seraph."

Raifen started to walk to his room when Seraph stopped him.

"Raifen, you're not going to bed yet until you have filled your stomach with some food. You'll need your strength tomorrow." Raifen seemed to have just remembered the food and gladly listened to his uncle. After a few minutes of stuffing his hungry face, Raifen gradually made his way to his bedroom.

"Good night, son," Seraph spoke.

"You too," replied a now tired Raifen.

Raifen, with ease and care, shut his door and walked to his bed. The room was dark except for the wax candle by the bedside that his uncle had laid there. It was shooting barely-visible rays of light to the far corner of the room, casting monstrous shadows along the plastered walls. The room had an unusual chill about it.

Raifen shuddered when first entering, a chill running down his spine and to his feet and back up to his head. He quickly undressed and jumped under the freshly washed bed sheets. The warmth returned to his limbs and Raifen lay for a few minutes reliving the events of the day. Sleep was drawing near to him. The last thing he remembered thinking was bits and pieces of the riddle the Nazracs had left for him to solve:

With you always big or small, in a child while he crawls, it is everywhere. Look in the heart and let it happen, you decide, you are captain, see it as it is, it is truth, it is his.

As the last words twirled in his head, he finally let go and fell into a deep, much needed sleep.

Part Two: The Journey

The young man stood clenching his stomach. The recent blow had knocked the air out of him. Apparently he had underestimated his opponent. He, too, was quick and strong, but the man knew he could beat him. Besides, the *Atem des Todes* had told him so. The hunched over man looked up, sneering at his opponent. The one who thought he had just laid the finishing blow, but he was mistaken. The man on the ground pretended to be hurting, keeping his head slouched. The other man circled around him. Teasing and laughing at him.

"You thought you could beat me, did you? Ha. How stupid can you be?" spoke the standing man. The other on the ground did not answer. He merely stayed how he was, lying as if defeated.

"Oh, brave boy. To think you could come into my house and have your way with her. Were you out of your mind?" The man rushed forward and kicked the man on the ground hard in the ribs. The man groaned, but still remained there. He smiled knowingly. She had been good. Far better than any other he had taken before. He made no move as to attack. Sometimes, the best offense is to let the enemy think you are injured, letting him bite at you repeatedly, and then attack when he thinks you are not capable. This was the plan of the man on the ground. He knew all too well what pain was, and this, this mere kicking and belittling from the other was nothing compared to what he had endured. No, the man knew what pain really was and he would be pleased when he inflicted it on his enemy.

"See. Look at you. You can't even stand. And you call yourself a man. You're nothing but a little coward. A *boy*."

The man on the ground peered up through his dangling hair, a look of pure hatred radiating in his eyes. The man standing up did not see this though, but instead thought he had hit a nerve with his last statement. He didn't know how right he was.

"Don't like that word, do you?" laughed the man. "Boy. Boy. *Boy…* "

It had been so sudden and unexpected that the man had not even known what was happening until his body lay dead on the dirt. The killer stood over his kill, snickering.

"How dare you speak of which you do not know," hissed the killer. "You shall join the rest of your foul kind soon enough. You are welcome, for I saved you the trouble of doing so yourself." The man spit into the face of the dead man, his mocker. He looked up. There was the sound of more men coming toward him. He could hear the wails of the dogs as they rushed forth through the trees, trailing his scent. The man cursed, hissing in displeasure, and yet, pleasing satisfaction. He looked down at the lifeless figure on the ground one last time, then left. He ran hurriedly through the trees, rushing ahead of his attackers. He knew this forest well, better than they, and so he came upon his little abandoned fortress of twigs that he called his home long before they found their dead companion. He shot forth through the dangling branches that barred the entrance. Once inside his sanctuary, his home from home, he began scrabbling through all the things inside. Papers, books, expensive jewels, and all sorts of meaningless things he had taken from his enemies. His mind went crazy and he slammed his fist on the small broken table, cursing aloud.

"Where is it," he fumed. And again he began throwing everything out of his way. He picked up the stool in the corner and threw it against a tree close by, splintering it into a thousand pieces. He brushed the thought of it aside, the thing was meaningless to him anyways. He had no use for it except to vent his frustrations, and these he did so exceedingly well, despite his still rather young age. He went to throw another pointless item, but stopped. He ran to the entrance of his lair. They were close. He cursed again. Dropping the item in his hands he began to search more frantically. Sweat began to form on his forehead, dripping into his eyes, blinding him momentarily and adding to his frustration. There was the sound of men close by now, as if they were not a few hundred feet away. There was no time. He would have to leave and come back later to search for it. He hated the mere thought of leaving without it. He felt incomplete without its touch. But he had no choice. The men could be there any moment now and he did not wish to be caught.

In the beginning, when he had first escaped the prison, the asylum as a little boy, the only fear was of going back if he were caught. But now, five years older, he would have much more demanding punishments set upon him. Not to mention since he had stolen count-less items and had his way with many of the wives and daughters of the men in town. This last thing was one of his favorites. One of the more demanding punish-ments was death. Death was something he did not wish for himself, but for others. He would not allow himself to be caught only so they could drag him to the center of the town and hang him for all to see, ravaging and torturing him the whole time until he begged for death. No, he would never allow that to come to pass. The man stepped outside, readying to leave. He was now just on the outskirts of the forest when he stopped and turned back around. He sprinted from the trees back to his home of foliage. When he was younger, and had first heard the voice, he thought himself mad. So many years later the voice was still unmistakable. He rushed forth into the hole that was used as the opening and began rummaging about the debris on the floor yet again. He knew the men were closer now and that they could at any moment come barging through the trees and surround him, finding him unprepared, but he did not care now. His master had called him and he would obey.

"I see you were going to leave without me," the voice said.

The man flinched, shuddering though he wished not. He began to speak in hollowed tones.

"I was merely going away for a time. Not to leave," answered the man. "I would never leave without you. You are the only means for which I still wish to live."

"As it should be," said the voice.

"Where are you?" the man demanded.

"Here."

The man began searching where the voice had answered, but still he couldn't find it.

"Here."

He snapped his head around and searched from where the voice had just been uttered. But still, he did not find it.

"Here." This time the voice seemed to be right on top of the man. The man did not know what to think about this last outburst.

"Here." The voice echoed softly inside his head.

"I am here." The man placed his hand against his head.

"Here?" he asked, feeling with his fingers around his scalp.

"Yes."

Then it hit him. He reached into his pocket then and there it was. The thing he had become so life-depending upon. Its cool surface sent chills through the man's body, but he welcomed this sensation. An energy throbbed throughout his body, granting him power. The artifact was one of magic, and its wielder would be granted those powers. Alas, the energy that pulsed through his veins even now. His eyes were closed when the men finally arrived. He did not even bother with their unwelcome presence until they awoke him from his inner ecstasy.

"Come out, beast from Dalek. We know you're

in there. Show yourself so that we might give you the honor of returning you to your homeland," yelled a man from outside. The man inside did not move.

"Here," the voice urged him to stay calm, to allow the others to make the first move, the wrong one.

"Look," began one of the other men outside, "he is too afraid to show himself."

"Coward," he yelled and all the others cheered with him, adding their own curses. The man inside was raging with anger. His fists were clinched and the sweat on his forehead was evaporating from the searing heat of hatred that he now felt.

"Here."

The voice relaxed him, but not fully.

"You shall have your wish soon enough," growled the man, through clenched teeth. "Soon."

The men outside now looked at one another. One was telling the others to go around back and that he and two others would go to the front. The men moved quietly to their positions as the one man kept yelling.

"See now," he began, "we only wish to take you into town and have your intestines for supper and to feed your scraps to our dogs. And if there is anything left over, to hang your corpse in the streets so that all can see what a true devil looks like."

The man inside knew of what they were doing. Though, they could not see him, he could see them. He had built the place for that specific reason, just in case someone dared to come bothering him. Two men were now behind him, and two more were on the sides. He couldn't help but let escape a snicker from his mouth. They didn't know what they were up against. The man in charge motioned with his hands for two of the men to circle to the front and go inside. On his signal, they were to do so. The two men hesitantly did so. Neither of them wanted to go in first, let alone by themselves. They were brave and tough men, but there was something about this fellow known as Yul that neither wished to come in contact with. He was known to be a deadly killer and a demon birthed from Dalek itself. Yul remained crouched inside, awaiting the approach of the two men. He knew how they played this game, but he would play it more cunning than they. He crept towards the back of the foreclosure and hid in the shadows.

"Yes."

The voice was pleased with his understanding and skill. He had come a long way since he first discovered it in the store. It had called to him then and had been teaching him for years its evil ways. The time had come to end this little game. These men were ignorant to the power he wielded and he wished to demonstrate it in full for their mindless brains. The first man entered, then the other. Both men came on slowly, unsure of what lay inside. Neither of them saw him crouched in the shadow of the corner, and neither of them saw him approach. He was so quick and so skilled in his attack that not even a scream came from the two men as he ended their lives. The blade dripped with their warm blood, shimmering red in the darkness from the use of its magic. Blood gushed from the hole in the one man's chest. The other had fallen over on his back, allowing his blood to soak the ground. Both men's eyes were frozen, displaying the shock that they felt when the blade had entered, instantly knowing that their lives were over. Neither could breathe. Their necks had been snapped as well, their lungs punctured in a fraction of a second. Yul stood up and walked toward the door.

"Abrim—Micah? Is he in there?" yelled the man. He was about to say something else but had not the chance. His breath was lost to him. All that his body allowed was for his mouth to droop. The scene that unraveled in front of him left him speechless. He had to be dreaming. There was no other explanation for it. Yul stood in the opening of the door. It was not the mere sight of him, but what he held in both his hands. The man choked, hurling right there on himself. Yul laughed.

"He is," answered Yul for the men, his evilness grinning through his smile and eyes. He tossed the two disembodied heads of the men he had just killed. They rolled to a stop, spilling their blood at the man's feet. The man stood in shock, his eyes displaying the terror, the pure horror he now was experiencing. His whole face looked white as if he had just seen the supernatural. And that he had.

"You've come for me?" asked Yul grinning. "Haven't you?"

The man said something that sounded like gibberish.

"As I thought," answered Yul, not paying attention to the man's lack of speech.

"Here I am," spoke Yul. "Are you going to take me in?" he mocked, acting like he were being taken a hold of and wrapped in chains. He mimicked the motion of being dragged. He tried to act pathetic, but found his acting skills weren't as well developed as his killing. He would have to be sure to fix that later. But now he would have a little fun.

"So," he started, walking back and forth in front of his house. "Who wants to be first?" Yul looked around for volunteers. There were none. And as he had expected, the other two men that were supposed to have been standing behind him on the side of his home, were now gone. He turned back around to face the man, a sadistic smile radiating on his face.

"Looks like it's just me and you," laughed Yul and he walked toward the man. The man began to whimper, begging for his life. He should have used those last breaths for something more meaningful, like prayer to the gods for help. Yul knew they wouldn't answer.

The two other men were now running as fast as they could. Upon seeing the demon they had come for, they lost all sense of courage and ran. Both were tiring, but neither wanted to stop. They had gone a few hundred feet into the woods when they both had stopped. Their faces showed their fear and they both began to run even faster. The scream behind them was heart-wrenching. The demon had killed their leader. His screams echoed all around them, not allowing them escape from its torment. They had to get away. This was an evil place. They could feel the death all around them.

Yul did not bother to wipe off his blade. There was already a perfect mix of three different bloods on it; he didn't want to spoil the taste for the other two. His hand glowed in the spoil of power that the blade granted him. It made him stronger, faster, quicker, smarter and more agile and able than any man or creature that lived. It gave him supernatural powers. One of which to know things that others would never know. Like the secrets of the earth and the power that it kept hidden. He would have it one day, but for now, he would be satisfied with the killings. He left, disappearing into the woods. He knew where they were going, but they would never make it. He left the body of the ravaged man behind him. He had enjoyed the kill more than he had the two previous ones. The man's screams had energized Yul, granting him a pleasure unknown of and rarely felt. It had been so invigorating that his pants now hung wet from the spill of emotion. Blood marked his entire body, but he did not mind. The man he had just killed was a lucky one. He had given him more time than the others. He had even taken the time to carve a design with his parts. Even now its curves stained the ground red. The star hex would be a remembrance for anyone who dared trespass into these woods.

The two men had to stop. Both were out of breath.

Breathing hard, gasping for air, they leaned against a tree. One leaned his head against the oak and peered up into the overhanging branches, looking at the blue that floated above them. As he noticed, there were no animals in these woods. Not a sound of life. The reason came soon enough. The man against the tree squealed in terror and shot off, now running again. The man that was left behind did not know what happened. The little hesitation he allowed was more than Yul needed. The man running ahead looked back over his shoulder several times, to make sure it wasn't following him. He regretted it once he did. Behind him, he watched as his friend was sliced into pieces right where he had been. Tears burst free from their tear ducks. Not out of sadness, but out of pure hopeless horror. He knew he was going to die. He just didn't want to.

Back by the tree, Yul let the limp body fall to the ground. The tree was splashed with blood and his blade now had another taste on its hinge. There was just one more and the circle would be complete. Yul stalked off after his prey.

The final scream came not long later. And then there was silence. The *Atem des Todes* had its share of flesh for the day. Five different tastes to be exact. It was ironic what the blade called itself. *Atem des Todes*. Breath of Death.

Memories of Vlandrax Xen

Eggs, Bacon, Bread

And here it shall begin. The beginning to the end. But first comes the end, then his sin, then the beginning back to the end. The ending is not clear, muted by the times of life. If we were any stronger than we are now, we could fight back. But alas, we are not. We are a weak race. Weak-minded, short-tempered, and ill advised in many things. If we had but one brave soul in this world that thought correctly, we could be devastating. But alas, we have neither. At one point, we did come close, but that was a time long ago. Though if there could have been something different he chose, things possibly could have been different, much different.

FROM THE SCROLLS OF DERACY

"Wake up Raifen, it's time to go," said Seraph.

Raifen didn't budge. It was chillier in the room now than it was the night before. He wanted to just stay under the warm covers. Raifen curled up into a little cotton ball and started to call sleep back to him. But with his uncle still pestering him to get a move on, he finally gave in and swung himself over the edge of the bed. Throwing the sheets off he quickly grabbed his nightgown and slipped into his slippers. It was a lot chillier than he remembered.

"It rained all night, if you're wondering why it still seems to be not yet dusk. The storm had just receded not an hour ago. It's pretty nasty outside. I think we might have to wait until it clears up a bit before taking off. I made you breakfast if you're hungry," explained Seraph.

"Thanks, Uncle," replied Raifen, grateful for his uncle's kindness.

Raifen walked out to the kitchen right away, being subdued into the aroma of eggs and buttered bread, along with some bacon and a glass of milk. Bestrow was barking happily as Raifen came into the kitchen. Bestrow could smell the delicious human food right above his head. It had to be even more painful for Bestrow, for being half beagle and all his nose was probably killing him with desire. Raifen scooped up a few eggs and bacon, grabbed two or three pieces of bread, and sat down to enjoy the well-cooked breakfast. Bestrow, now drooling, couldn't help but to follow in hopes that Raifen might sneak him some scraps of food, like he normally did. The eggs were nice and round; moisture seeped through the cracks of Raifen's fork. The bacon was thick and crunchy and the bread was baked to perfection. A now impatient Bestrow began to whine for the hope to soften his master's heart. Raifen patted his oversized hound on the head, teasing him with some bread while waving it around so that Bestrow's seeking eyes would follow it and then quickly stuffing it into his mouth, causing a whine to come from Bestrow. Bestrow's tail wagged happily each time he thought he was going to get some food, but only ended with disappointment. Raifen finally couldn't take the pleading eyes looking at him and he gave Bestrow some of his bacon and half a slice of bread.

"You better not be feeding that dog," started Seraph,

but with a curling smile on his lips. "He's fat enough as it is."

"Oh no, course not, just a little bacon and a piece of bread. I don't see any food to feed Bestrow with. All gone," replied Raifen innocently smirking.

"Well if you're all done then, wash up and get your stuff together, we need to make a move before daybreak," continued Seraph, as if his joking had not even been of subject just a few moments ago. Raifen got up and washed his plate and went to his room to get his things together before the long journey. Bestrow remained behind, under the table licking his lips and smelling around on the floor for some crumbs he might have possibly missed.

NEW REVELATION

Raifen's stomach protruded a little from his shirt. He had eaten enough food to last him a whole week, though in mild proportions. He opened up his closet and pulled out an old sack that had been given to him by his uncle as a gift. He would not have thought of this bag as anything special but for the fact it belonged to his father, it being the only real thing he had that held any sense of remembrance of his father. He had never known his father and he had cherished the day when his uncle had given it to him.

He held it in his arms for a few seconds, his mind wandering to a time when he might have been able to see his father. Those days would never come, though he wished for them to. He pulled open his cabinet and began the laborious job of stacking all his clothes into piles to be placed into the sack. He had merely a dozen or so shirts, with three to four pairs of slacks. He emptied the cabinet in no time.

While packing his articles of clothing into his sack, Raifen came across a frame lying on his desk. It had drawn his eyes to it, though he never remembered looking at the desk. *That wasn't there before,* he thought. He gradually picked it up, thoroughly examining its diagram, frame and all. It turned out to be some kind of magical scene of a family. But it was strange. Scenes could only be transferred into frozen glances by using magic. And magic didn't exist, did it? Raifen couldn't believe he was holding a magical item. A frozen scene that was only make-believe. As he looked closer he realized it was his family, taken when his mother was still alive and his father had not yet disappeared. But, there was someone else in the scene that Raifen had never seen before. It was a boy. He himself hadn't been born yet so it couldn't have been him in the scene. He was curious and quickly flipped the framing over to the backside. There he found he had been right. It was his family. But it was strange when he saw the small print naming who all was there. The boy had a name that sounded familiar though Raifen had never actually heard it before. But still, it held something unusual about it, maybe it was just how the framed scene made him feel, looking into the past in a way, seeing his mother and father for the first time, though the second time now seeing his mother, since he had just had a dream about her the other night in the mysterious, magical place she called, Amaranth. The boy's name, as read said: "Kibitzer Genesis."

Kibitzer? Genesis? Could this be? Did he have a brother? The questions were still going through his head as he finished packing and walked out to stack his stuff up in the wagon outside, where his uncle was at the moment.

He would ask his uncle about the magical scene when he saw him, he assured himself.

DEPARTURE

While his nephew was getting his stuff ready, Seraph was keeping himself busy making sure the horses' harnesses were nicely fastened and secure for their trip ahead. Checking one last time to make sure all the animals were cooped up in their little huts, Seraph begins loading the wagon. Just then the front door opens and down comes Raifen, a puzzled look on his face. With him carrying his large duffel bag over his right shoulder, but in his other free hand, holding something that looked to be a magically frozen scene of some kind.

"All ready to go?" asked Seraph.

"Just about, Uncle," replied Raifen. He hesitated at first to speak his thoughts, not sure how his uncle would react. He decided he would take the chance and asked.

"Uncle," he began, "Did I have a brother at one time?" His words caused a curious look to come to his uncle's face. Seraph continued to load the wagon, seemingly ignoring Raifen's question, but Raifen waited patiently for his uncle to finish. Seraph acted like nothing was bothering him, but inside his mind was racing. He had known that one day or another Raifen would have some questions about his life, but this early on was pushing things. He had not been ready for it. After throwing the last bag into the back of the wagon, he jumped down and wiped the sweat that started to gather along his forehead.

"A brother you ask? Yes, of course you had one, but he

decided he would take off to his homeland instead of 'waiting here for the end to come to us all,' by his words. A disgrace he was to his family. We didn't want to tell you that you had a coward for a brother. So we kept it a secret from you until we thought you should know," explained Seraph.

"This scene then, it's my brother?" asked Raifen. He pointed to the boy in the photo.

"Yes. That's him. When your mother was dying she told me to watch over you for her, to protect you, and to keep the truth from you as long as was necessary to do you unnecessary harm. I kept the knowledge of your brother with me for eighteen years after your mother died. And that scene you now hold in your hand."

"Why didn't you say anything before to me?" persisted Raifen.

"I didn't want you to know of your brother and his sins and betrayal to his father and mother. I—*we*—thought that it would be better if you didn't know right away, for it might have disappointed you. We didn't want you to follow in his and your father's footsteps and run away from your problems like they did. I kept my word to your mother. I didn't tell you anything until I thought you should know. That's why I placed that frozen scene on your desk, in hopes that you would see it lying there, and have the curiosity to pick it up. I thought that this was a good time for you to learn of your brother before we headed out to Petipala. Many truths lie ahead of you. Some you may not wish to believe, others, you may find hard to. I'm sorry that I didn't tell you sooner, but I gave my word to your mother. I hope you will forgive me, for your mother's sake."

Seraph looked away. Though he felt sad for keeping the truths from his nephew, he still felt he needed to keep his promise to his sister. It was the least he could do for her. Raifen forgot about the fact that his uncle hadn't told him earlier about his brother for his chest started to burn. Reddish-purple hues started to wrap themselves around his body. Chest first, working their way down his legs and back up to his head. Through the pain he seemed to see a thick forest. The forest came in and out of view. He had an unusual feeling that he knew this place.

Was it—is it? Yes, it has to be, thought Raifen to himself.

"Raifen, Raifen, what's wrong? What is it," a frightened Seraph asked while seeing his nephew submerged in reddish-purple colors. But the words were mere soft voices, acute sounds drifting through a barrier that hindered its structure.

Finally, Seraph grabbed his nephew just as he started to collapse, wrapping him in a blanket. Raifen, dazed, looked up at his uncle. Seraph had heaved him up onto the wagon and now sat next to him. He laid him on the bench so that he wouldn't fall down. Seraph snapped the reins of the horses, the journey now on the way. Raifen was dozing off again. He tried to fight off the sudden sense of exhaustion, but he failed. There was nothing else he could do; he let it take hold of him. He found himself sliding through a river of tunnels, all black and lifeless, as he slipped into the realm of shadows.

AM I DREAMING?

The same forest seemed to loom right in front of him now. Was he awake or was he dreaming again? Raifen knew not the difference between the two. He was floating in a far from real world. Every now and then the woods and the smog that was guarding the forest seemed to go in and out of focus. Every time when coming back into focus, Raifen would be even closer to this sanctuary. Raifen was drawn to this barren wasteland of broken underbrush, fallen trees, lifeless, the looming quietness consuming every step he took. Raifen had a strange sense of comfort when walking into the woods. The woods were welcoming him and not condemning him to death and telling him to leave. It was as if they were urging him on. The trees seemed to talk in whispers, whispering to one another, through a language that Raifen had never heard of before, every now and then catching a name, his name. Raifen thought he heard his name being chanted. The trees were saying, "P-pol-ly-an-na, come with us. Don't stop, follow the ancestors' voices."

Raifen had no choice but to follow, the rhythmic sounds were somehow hypnotizing him, filling his heart with a kind of hormone. Raifen felt good all over, a sense of satisfaction, as a child would be when accomplishing something thought impossible to achieve. Raifen was not only being drawn toward the center of the woods core, but rather, he was going willingly. The voices started up again, but in a different tune this time, speaking, "g-g-oo-o tooo h-im-m, go-o Pol-l-lya-nnn-aa, he-e wa-i-i-tts-s att Ma-a-rr-o-ww."

Raifen couldn't make out the rest of what they were saying, sounded as if they all started yelling or another. Raifen walked a little closer toward the voice that was screaming loudest, until he was hit by something in the head. The visions started to die out and turn to an over-powering black.

SECRETS

Raifen's eyes sprung open with vigor. They were now on the road far away from Sol. As he turned his head to look back from where they came, a cold shiver seeped in his body. The feeling that this might be the last time he saw this place haunted his feelings. He was on a bigger adventure than he had ever imagined. Where it led he did not know. But one thing, he was leaving home. The buildings of Sol were now just little gray specks in the distance. He had slept a long time. Trees, trees, and more trees now surrounded them. All sorts of trees, oak, fern, spruce, pine, it was there. But among all of these trees one stood out the most, the Safewood Forest, the vastest and most devouring woods all around. People used to make for the Safewood Forest to gain safety from the Bringer of Death's villains. The Talions and Fangeors used to abandon the task of gathering the ones who ran into the forest. To go in the Safewood Forest was to vow an oath of no return, for Safewood was almost inescapable. The Talions and Fangeors were fearful of getting lost in the woods and they left the humans to their own deaths.

"Have a nice nap, young one?" smirked Seraph.

Raifen was rubbing his head, where a bump was beginning to form shape.

"Oh, sorry about the bump, I went to tap you awake and hit a ditch in the road and hit you harder than I wanted to," explained Seraph, trying to put a truthful expression on his face.

Raifen didn't believe him fully but didn't worry too much about it. He couldn't remember much about his dream. *So it was a dream then,* thought Raifen. "Uncle, where are we now?"

"We are a few days ride from Blasa." He saw the look on his nephew's face and followed it to where it stared at the forest up ahead. A small grin crossed his face, a little distraught. "That is the Safewood Forest, if you are wondering." Raifen didn't even look up at his uncle. Recognition formed on his brow and he continued to stare unwaveringly. There was something about this forest that drew Raifen towards it.

"It is told that this is where people ran for safety from the Bringer of Death," continued Seraph, as if Raifen had urged him for more information regarding the whereabouts and knowing of the forest.

"People believed that our ancestors had once put an enchantment on the place, allowing it to protect its fellow beings. Also, it is told that the forest whispers to itself. Sometimes calling people into it, and they who listen to its call, never return again."

"What happens to them Uncle?" asked Raifen.

"Well, it is said that they who contain the bloodline of the one are normally the ones who it calls; and that whoever listens to it, winds up getting lost in the Marrow," continued Seraph.

Raifen was remembering what the voices were saying in the forest, the place where they said "he was waiting," whoever "he" was.

"The Marrow?"

"It's the heart of Safewood, meaning where the strength resides and is the pith of the whole forest."

"I've heard of it."

"You have? From who?"

"Oh, just the other teenagers in town," lied Raifen.

He wasn't sure he wanted to tell his uncle about his dream just yet. He still wanted to figure out who this "he" was that the voices were talking about. The Safewood Forest was some fifteen feet away when Seraph ordered the horses to halt.

"I think we traveled far enough today Raifen."

The sun was almost dispersed in clouds on the western planes. Sunset was no doubt taking hold. The moon already was making its way to its throne in the night sky. Stars were popping into view all over the darkened sky, in unison with the universe's wishes. The nocturnal animals were already starting their wakening sounds. Coyotes howled to the moon, hoping to gain favor with their king, to give them the power to hunt that night, or else go hungry. Night crawlers made safe passage through their newly formed terrain. Locust sang songs to one another, in hopes of gaining a female's attention. Bull frogs relieved themselves of the gas built up all day. The forest was a wonder to look at during the nighttime. There was something about it, like it was casting a spell over you. A light breeze was blowing while the fire Seraph was building was taking form. A few moments passed and Raifen joined his uncle. Neither talked much that night being exhausted from the long day. Both just went to sleep without much conversation with each other. Sleep nagged at Raifen while he lay thinking

MATTHEW THRUSH

about the whispers coming from the woods. The sound of his uncle clearly having fallen asleep could be heard from the low whooshes of the air being passed out of his lungs. Raifen soon followed suit and was hardly asleep when ...

TOSSING AND TURNING

I t was a quiet night with the exceptions of the occasional cry of a coyote. The locust had stopped singing and the bullfrogs no longer were out croaking. A damp mist crept out from the forest's edge. You could taste the water vapor in the air. More or less it was like a giant smog devouring the land with its magnificence. Raifen and Seraph were sound asleep now, the fire burning low in the dim light. Raifen was having a hard time sleeping. He kept tossing and turning throughout the night, only to be awakened by his own screaming.

A Voice is Silent

R aifen, Raifen."

An easing voice was whispering into his ear.

"Don't listen to it, remember what Seraph said, 'the ones who listened, we never see again.'"

Raifen struggled with all his might not to slip into that soothing melody gently calling his name. Raifen didn't know how long he could take it; it was getting to him. That same voice asking again for him to follow, but this time it was more like it was demanding him to come.

Can't Seraph hear that, thought Raifen. *Of course he can't you fool, he isn't in the bloodline of the Genesis.*

Someone was speaking to Raifen in the language of the woods. Raifen felt like he knew the person.

"Who are you? What do you want from me? Why are you calling me?" he asked.

Again that same voice urged him, trying to subdue him to its will. Raifen thought that the whispers talked back and were saying to come and learn everything. Raifen realizing that they meant him no harm, released himself to follow and to go with the spirits.

For what else could these voices be, he thought. What harm could they do to him? He wasn't touching them, was he? No. The mental connection broke and he was left there, sitting, thinking about what the voices had promised him.

Great rewards and treasures, they said. Valuable notes, mysteries, and secrets are to be told. Come to us and we shall give you all these. And more. Raifen was more than curious enough to dwell on the subject for hours. He knew something was wrong with the way he could hear the forest speaking, but he also thought it to be strange, rather peculiar that he, a human, could hear the forest talk, and as a gift or a blessing from them that he had the honor. And not just hear them, but talk back. There was something hidden in the walls of the forest, some secret kept hidden from the eyes of strangers. But he was being welcomed and greeted. Should he abide by their wishes and accept? Or would he, in not accepting their charity, be forbidden to cross and to never return to this place? He knew the stories of how the forest could be wicked. He did not wish for his lack of understanding to guarantee his failure. He would see what they wanted. He would go. His answer would mark the beginning of his destiny, though he knew not the full extent of his choice. One day he may, but not yet.

FORGIVENESS IN THE
FORM OF REGRET

The woods were more dense and murky than they appeared from outside the wood. There was so much more thicket and shrubbery than Raifen had ever been in. The trees were sticking to one another. The woods gave off a claustrophobic feeling and there was barely enough space for Raifen to maneuver through. At times he thought he would get stuck, but he always managed to get through. He began to think that the trees were swinging out of his way as he walked along. He had an uneasy feeling of many eyes staring at him from all over. The same voice continued to encourage him along, but there were other voices now. The trees or whatever they were, were all talking in whispers. Raifen had a funny feeling that he was the topic. The trees began to converge to one single opening up ahead. Raifen emerged through a crevice in the branches only to be replaced by the trees arms. The plants seemed to cover the place he had just come through.

"So that's why people can never get out, they don't know which way they came in from. They don't know which way is the right way."

Raifen went a few more steps, and then the voice stopped calling him. He wasn't scared or worried at all, he was filled with overflowing courage. The opening was low at first then rose to a centered point overhead. Even with Raifen's eyes accustomed to the obscured surroundings, this basin was more concealed with darkness, except for the occasional rays of light making their way through the forest's top. Through the dimness, Raifen could see a figure crouched down next to a fairly large rock. He seemed to be humming to himself. The rhythm of the syllables were recognizably the same as the one's that led Raifen here.

"Hello, Raifen. I have been waiting for you."

"Have you now?"

"Yes. Do you know who I am?"

It was hard for Raifen to recognize any definite features through the blinding darkness.

"No. Step into the light so I can see you."

The figure shifted a little uneasily on the rock, his invisible head seeming to rotate towards Raifen's direction.

"Come out so I can see your face," Raifen said, starting to get more fervent with his patience running out.

"An impatient one, are you? Can't wait for the man to gather his bearings after being run in on by an unexpected visitor?"

"You're the one who called me here. Can't let a fellow catch his bearings," Raifen mocked. "He calls me here and doesn't have the decency to explain. Oh, I am not going to stand here and take it, no sir." He didn't have time for this nonsense.

"If you persist."

"I do."

"Very well then."

He stood up, clearly having trouble. Raifen felt no empathy for the man.

"He deserves it the no good excuse for a human."

The figure stepped into the light. Raifen's mouth

dropped. Standing in front of him was none other than the boy in the frozen scene, his brother, of course with the consideration of the years of the past and the many scars along his cheeks and arms. The marks of one who was ravished and beaten over and over again. The marks of great hardships and failures. Enticing to make one feel sorry for the man, but Raifen was not moved except for the first shock of seeing his brother for the first time in his life, so he thought.

"Kibitzer, how did you—"

"Quite a long story my brother, Raifen."

The look that crossed Kibitzer's face was not one of happiness, but of someone who has kept the growing tension of anger towards another for centuries. Kibitzer did not seem too enthused in seeing his brother, nor Raifen he.

"You seem shocked to see me, young one?"

Kibitzer, the first-born, was twelve when Raifen was born.

"Yes. I never thought it would be you I was talking to, I have but only just found out earlier today of your existence."

That would seem so, since I tried to kill you, thought Kibitzer to himself.

"That sounds like mother, all right. How is she these days?" a mocking Kibitzer asked—a question that he already knew the answer.

"She's dead."

The thought of never knowing his mother his whole

life, crept in Raifen's thoughts, but dispersed after what came next.

"Of course she's dead. She died bringing your disgraced body into this world."

An overwhelming feeling to chastise his brother for his unkindly words came over him, but he refrained from the human instinct to do so. Instead, he just continued to stare blankly at Kibitzer.

"Oh, so now he has nothing to say? Well, I do. Do you know what it's like to be locked up in this place? Do you have any idea in that little bitty skull of yours? Huh?"

"I could guess," Raifen said.

"You could guess? Baa. The one who is supposed to save us all can only guess. Well let me tell you, Raifen, how it is. It sucks. I hate always being awake. I hate never being able to find my way out, but always somehow finding my way back here. I hate the company. I've wasted eighteen years of my life in this god-forsaken place. I regret to have ever listened to the voices."

Kibitzer paused with his face buried in his hands. A now crying Kibitzer looked up at his brother.

"I wish I could be free. If I could do it all over again, I would." Kibitzer paused again to try and gain his composure.

"I'm sorry I ever tried to kill you my brother. I'm sorry." Kibitzer became unable to control his emotions any longer. Raifen was dumbfounded by the startling news. He watched and allowed his brother to grieve over his past; Raifen did not want to bring any disrespect to his brother.

MATTHEW THRUSH

"Could you somehow find it in your heart to forgive me?"

Raifen's scar started to sting. What Kibitzer hadn't realized by Raifen's stillness was that he had already forgiven him. The prophecy Raifen had not heard of, was being fulfilled to the last letter.

"I forgive you, Kibitzer."

Kibitzer looked up as if he had just seen an angel. The sparkle returned to his eyes and the face that had long since had a smile, was now smiling with unspeakable happiness.

"Thank you."

"You can thank me later. Right now we need to find a way out of here."

"I've tried for two decades. I'm sorry I can't help you there. The tales say that there is no way out."

"Oh, there is a way out, Kibitzer. Have faith."

Raifen's scar was burning even more now, the reddish-purple swirls of colors escaping from his cloak.

"What is happening, brother? Are you alright?"

"Fine, just my scar is hurting again. I think we should go this way. Follow me."

And with no further ado, Raifen disappeared into the trees, with Kibitzer on his heels.

EARLY MORNING FEAR

The morning was clear and warm with some clouds in the eastern part of the sky. The woods were now quiet and not a sound was to be heard. Seraph was up gathering wood to refuel the fire, preparing breakfast for when Raifen would return. Seraph was not sure what got into Raifen to leave in the middle of the night. Seraph didn't worry too much about it, he just figured Raifen got up before daybreak and went for a little stroll around the different forests. Seraph was beginning to get worried now. Raifen's absence was coming up on five hours. He had courage that his nephew could take care of himself, but the fatherly side of him was nagging at him.

UNRAVELING ESCAPE ROUTE

The forest was indeed how the tales had it, one could get easily lost in it if he weren't paying attention. Raifen was not about to let that happen to him and his newfound brother. The woods were much more at peace than they had been the previous night. It had been a day since Raifen had saved his brother from the Marrow. Kibitzer was beginning to become unbelieving of his brother's saying he could get them out, but keep following he did.

"Raifen?"

"Yes."

"It appears to me that we might be lost."

"Why would you think that, Kibitzer?"

"Well, you see those trees over there, near the dead river's side?"

"Yes."

"We have come past those same trees where the roots seem uprooted and by which no life seems to coexist. And that stone ledge over yonder? That is the same rock cliff in these parts that we have seemed to walk right by all day. We have been walking in circles, Raifen."

Raifen thought and looked at the places Kibitzer had just mentioned. His brother was right; they had been past those forest markings already and then some. Maybe they were going in circles. Raifen agreed to his brother's observations and decided that they were indeed going in circles. Raifen tried to focus on the task at hand and clear out all the excess material. He closed his eyes for a moment. When he opened them again, he looked around for a sign of difference, a sign of freedom. While looking closely at all the different tree hangings, dirt corruption, the sizes and shapes of the underbrush, a certain tree seemed to grab his attention. Kibitzer saw his brother going over to the tree, but didn't interrupt his brother's concentration. He believed in his brother. The tree was somewhat oval, and bent towards one side, with the other end twisting around itself. It didn't resemble any of the other woodwork in the forest, something was certainly odd about this one and Raifen knew it. While looking closely over the tree for any appearances of a corruption, he found it, a small dent in the trees base, invisible to the human eye, but of course Raifen wasn't looking through human eyes at present.

"Kibitzer, I think I found something."

Kibitzer ran over to where his brother was and bent over to look where his brother was pointing with his index finger. A puzzled look came upon Kibitzer. He was beginning to worry about his brother now.

"Can't you see the indention?"

"Raifen are you feeling okay, maybe we should rest for awhile?"

"No, I'm not seeing things, there is a little finger print of some animal or spirit, to mark the way out." The so-called fingerprint looked mighty similar to Raifen's scar. The same diamond shaped twisting of the skin with what looked like a hand pointing with one finger extended. Raifen pushed on this clue.

For what honestly looked like an ancient tree, the

bark or whatever material it was made of felt rubbery and yet more solid than steel to Raifen's touch. Nothing happened at first, but then the tree started to gently vibrate, its leaves falling off, flailing in the breeze like spider webs, a high-pitched squeal escaping from its markings. All the other trees now began joining in now. All of which were screaming invisible words at Raifen and his brother and blowing wildly as if in a great storm. Just as abruptly as it started, it stopped. All was quiet and still. All but the one tree which was still shimmering slightly. A glow perspired off of it, swirling to where Raifen now stood anxious and at the ready. Hues of white and black mixed with turquoise combined together to form one single, pure color. Raifen's scar was aching and spawning its reddish-purple colors towards the others, both meeting and rapidly consuming one another. It was quite a horrifying scene to someone who might have just walked in on it and not knowing the true affect of what was happening. Kibitzer was flabbergasted at the sight.

"What's happening Raifen?"

"I'm not too sure, but I think that there is some kind of spell over this tree and it's connecting with my power."

The firework of colors now had long dispersed. Raifen was staring quietly at the tree and the surrounding glooming plants. The forest began to fade away leaving three different passageways. One on the left, one on the right, and one somewhat in the middle. The one on the left side appeared more worn and walked on, nothing but dirt and mud, with footsteps of others who had walked that same path. The one opposite was lush with greens and flowers glistening in the light that came from it. This too had some footprints layered in the soil, but not as many as the other. An enticing aroma was stewing from this certain path, but Raifen still wasn't sure of it. Finally, the one centered almost congruent to the other two, was dark, threatening your life it appeared, whispers were crawling from its gloom. No footprints were to be seen. No flowers, no sweet scents, no lush grass to perch oneself upon, no, not one single thing that would entice the human soul to wonder into its abyss, but Raifen. He seemed to be drawn to it like he was to wander into the woods aimlessly only to find out it was his brother he would stumble upon. The same whispering voices grasping at Raifen's cloak.

"Think Raifen, think," he said with hands clasped around his face trying so desperately to focus on which path he and his brother should take. Raifen knew he and his brother were at stake if he chose the wrong one to follow. If he chose the right one, no one knew where it would take them.

"Show me the way. Show me which one is the way to follow—which one is out?"

A few seconds passed and the two with enticing footprints had vanished from Raifen's line of vision. Flames of color were evaporating off Raifen's chest; the last and final pathway stared blankly at him. The one more centered from the others. The one less tempting to pass through. The one that looked like it inflicted more pain. This is the one Raifen chose. Raifen's heart throbbed and tried to escape out of his chest. The mist of power and color streaming from his chest and body were already floating and drifting toward, and much was already within, the glooms of the forlorn trail.

"Let's go Kibitzer, it's time we got out of this forsaken place."

"Lead the way, oh thoughtful one." replied Kibitzer, making a joke of his brother's thought process.

And so they disappeared into the abyss. Small remnants of color remained a few temporal seconds later after both bodies dispersed into the darkness; they quietly and quickly, vanished. The opening closed. Nothing remained but the appearance of before—trees.

CURIOSITY—DOUBT

Back at the camp, Seraph had extinguished the fire's final flames and had finished gathering all the supplies together and packed them away in the back of the wagon. The sun was starting to shine brightly in the early afternoon, beaming down on the forest from above. Hardly a cloud was to be seen on this glorious day in the early spring. Flocks of birds were beginning to make their way from the sleeping winter in a far away land instilled with warmth back to the comfort of their true homes. Bestrow was barking at the far side of the trees, some hundred feet away from where the camp was situated.

"What is it boy? What do you smell?"

Bestrow wound his head around so he was looking at Seraph, and with some effort finally got Seraph to follow.

"Lead the way, boy. Show me what you found."

WHAT NEXT?

The forest trees weren't as thick and crowding as before, as if they were parting out of the way with every step Raifen took. The silent swoosh back and forth of the trees being blown by the invisible wind. Once and awhile a bird would screech and zoom at them out of nowhere and disappear just as suddenly. The trail wound sideways and then back again, forever winding itself around all the underbrush. It led them to a small stream with dreamingly clear frosty water. Raifen, for a moment, had thought he lost the trail, but still it loomed in front of them off to one side, still urging them on. The trail made another sudden and unexpected jolt to the left at about a ninety-degree angle, and Raifen and Kibitzer crashed through the trees that were straight ahead, missing the turn yet again.

"Curse this bloody trail," grimaced Kibitzer through a mouthful of dirt.

"Hush Kibitzer, the forest can hear you, we don't want it getting angry with us now, especially not with us so close to being out."

Kibitzer quickly agreed not wanting to stay any longer in this Dalek like dungeon.

Follow, this way.

"You heard it, let's go," ushered Raifen.

Brushing the newly formed dirt off their cloaks, they made for the new turn. They hadn't gone more than fifty feet when another unexpected obstacle hit them. A seemingly straight drop-off now pulled at their off-balanced bodies. Kibitzer, luckily with Raifen's sudden shout of warning, had grabbed a branch and quickly grabbed his brother before he fell to what could have possibly been death. The drop went down and down and still down, past the limit the eye could see, ending in darkness. Panting and trying to gain breaths through their startled hearts, Raifen and Kibitzer lay on the damp ground just narrowly escaping their deaths yet again.

"This couldn't possibly get any worse?" stated Kibitzer looking over his shoulder at his brother. "Oh, I'm quite certain it could," Raifen paused, hearing something. "And I think it just has."

Raifen quickly jumped to his feet dragging Kibitzer by the arm and at the same time turning to see the trees straining to hold against an unknown force.

"I think we had better make a run for it," Raifen said.

Kibitzer, seeing what his brother was looking at, made no argument about it. He didn't have to be told twice, he was running before Raifen had ever given it thought. Twisting and winding their way through this maze of branches trying desperately to escape the oncoming traffic of what sounded like a herd of animals on a stampede. They didn't want to have the opportunity to confirm their theory. Tripping and sliding the whole way down the narrowing passage. The noise was getting closer. It was gaining on them, they needed to go faster.

MATTHEW THRUSH

QUESTIONING THOUGHTS

Back at the camp, Seraph was following Bestrow to see what he was all worked up about. Not taking any chances, he brought his bow with him, with an arrow already notched on and ready to be sent flying at any sudden movement. Seraph stopped some ten feet away from the opposing forest, and listened intently on an almost mute sound. Bestrow stopped barking and that worried Seraph quite a bit. It was uncommon for Bestrow to stop barking. Cocking the bow string back even further, he took a few steps closer. The sound was now more recognizable and closer at that.

What was happening? He wondered.

An Enemy but
Friend at His Hand

Hurry Kibitzer, it's gaining on us."

"You try sitting in the Marrow for eighteen years and you see how you react to running a marathon all at once. I'm sorry, Raifen, but I was not made for this kind of movement." Even in the midst of danger they both seemed to have a sense of humor.

"Yeah, I agree, you weren't made to be a cross-country runner," said Raifen with sarcasm. In spite of what was happening, Kibitzer managed a smile. They had only some thirty feet separating them from the noise behind them now.

"Look! Up ahead. An opening," yelled Raifen.

The forest seemed it was coming to an end only ten feet away now. They burst through, jumped over a fallen log and were now in the opening, but it wasn't an opening at all, it was a small field, a continuation of the forest. Kibitzer cursed under his breath.

Kibitzer and Raifen stopped for a brief rest to catch their breaths.

"How far do you reckon it is?" asked Raifen.

He dared a look back at the opposing enemy and that's when he saw what was after them, a horde of birds, birds of all shapes and sizes, crashing and making their way through the forbidden forest, to what it appeared, seeking to bring destruction to him and his brother.

MATTHEW THRUSH

"I'd say about three hundred yards, more or less," answered Kibitzer.

"No time for anymore discussion, we're still being hunted."

"I thought we lost it when we came out here?"

"Supposedly not, we have an army of birds chasing us down. We better move while we still have a head start."

Again they began running. The field was smooth and flat and offered no resistance to their steps as they ran. The opposite side of the forest, which was now behind them burst into flames of birds, black winged beasts marked with the darkness that consumed them in the woods. They were almost to the other side, but now that these beasts were out in the open they loomed ever faster upon them, gaining and removing the distance between them with every stroke of wings.

"Faster Kibitzer, they're gaining on us again."

"I'm trying, I'm trying. These legs will only move at a certain speed, no faster."

"We're almost there, just a little farther."

The screeching was now upon them and Raifen heard a scream, but one of a human being attacked. Raifen turned to see a few of the more cunning birds nipping at his brother. He ran full throttle at the oncoming army with the force of a hurricane and the courage of a tiger. The birds were now swarming around Kibitzer, devouring him amongst their beating wings.

"Stop," shouted Raifen. Running at them with his arms outstretched and a look of control and power in his eyes, those now darkened masses of dark green and blackened hues, shining with the fiery redness of the sun. A reddish mist spun around his body, encasing him in a shield of smoking power. It ran throughout his body, empowering him with ultimate control. The birds flickered and stumbled, and some of the weaker ones flew away, but the stronger, more rebellious ones stayed, flapping their wings in rebuke and yelling their bird-like curses at Raifen.

"I said leave him alone and disappear from my sight," spoke Raifen with utmost authority as a king over his people. The birds' composure changed. A once deceitful looking army, now a whimpering one, sought Raifen's sympathy.

"Go!" shouted Raifen again.

With not the hint of disobedience, their wings fluttered once, and they were gone, vanishing into the woods. Raifen walked over to his brother and helped him off the ground.

"Are you okay?"

Kibitzer brushed himself off and checked for signs of weakness.

"Yeah, just dandy, except for the fact I was swarmed by a cloud of fluttering beasts," Kibitzer laughed, "and luckily just a few scraps and cuts. Nothing too serious, but my manhood has been threatened."

Kibitzer tried to make out a little humor after the little affair he and his brother had just had with the woods' defense.

"How did you do that anyway?"

Raifen didn't answer. He may never answer that question. Raifen looked around for signs of lingering animals on the prowl. When finally thinking that all was safe and back to normal, or at least as normal as the woods would allow, he turned to Kibitzer.

"If everything is alright, I think we should continue on our way before those birds decide to make things even between us and them."

"Good idea."

A pained look worked its way in Kibitzer's eyes; he was not yet willing to relive the moment again. Not feeling completely satisfied with his brother's responses to his inquiries, Raifen turned and resumed in leading them through the final hundred feet through the wood's last opposing obstacle. The trees were less aggressive on the outer boundaries of the forest; thin, weak-looking trees widely separated from one another, less underbrush along the tree's base, more light and life appearing through the tops of the trees. This section of trees were worldlier; more normal and how trees were supposed to be. Birds were chirping happily, celebrating the new day to be spent with a joyous attitude and a determined sun above. Other animals like squirrels, rabbits, an occasional deer, were wandering through the woods with a not so set location of direction. Raifen smiled. Kibitzer was enjoying it more than Raifen. He chased after the squirrels, tried to grab falling birds and tried to sneak up on a doe at one point. He was having fun with his soon-to-be-freedom. Taking advantage of it before, for some reason, he found himself back in the Marrow or some other organic prison finding out it had all been a dream.

"Kibitzer! The forest is ending just up ahead. See, the trees are thinning and I can see the light seeping through."

Kibitzer who was just about to try and grab a woodpecker, came back to reality from his silly boyish acts. He ran to join Raifen.

"Just five more little steps and we're through," Raifen announced. Without waiting for his brother, Kibitzer ran the remaining length of trees and came storming out to a nervous looking and anticipating Seraph on the other side. A few moments later Raifen came bursting through the trees to find two people staring at one another with a non-peaceful look on their faces.

"Uncle, I see you found Kibitzer, or more like he found you."

"Yes Raifen, we have met before. I've heard plenty about him to know how he truly is."

"That's where I'm afraid you're wrong old man. I've changed and it seems you have too in one way or more."

Kibitzer was eying Seraph down, acknowledging the pockets under the worn down man he once knew.

"Looks like the years caught up with you, eh, Seraph?"

"You're not one to talk Kibitzer, you don't look too good yourself."

Raifen broke into the conversation before things got crazy. He stepped up to his uncle and began to explain how Kibitzer had been calling him to come into the woods and how he found him in the Marrow. He spoke about Kibitzer telling of another part of the prophecy, the one that curses him to remain in the Marrow until forgiven by the one he marked with his jealousy and anger. How Kibitzer had poured out his heart to Raifen asking for forgiveness. How he had forgiven him, then how they were finally able to escape the Safewood, a forest no one had gotten out of

MATTHEW THRUSH

until now. How he had fought off the wild beasts; more or less, how he had told them to leave. Raifen waited while all the information transferred into Seraph's head. When he was satisfied that he had caught up with the present, Raifen asked, "So?"

Seraph seemed to be thinking and having a hard time at it, appearing to be struggling within himself, maybe over pride or for loathing his nephew he had been welling up all these years. His mind, wielding and exaggerating more and more on things that never happened, until the truth was blinded from him; he was living a lie.

"How did you come to find him here?"

"He was in the Marrow. He called to me with the songs of the trees he had learned over the years. Eighteen years, to be certain."

"But what on earth, Kibitzer, were you doing in the Marrow?"

A cocky look came upon Kibitzer's brow.

"I did not go there on my own whim. I was cursed to the place, banned from all human contact and worldly life."

"And rightfully so, you deserved to be forsaken to the awful place for the sins you had tried to comment," Seraph said.

"Yes, I know about our past and I do not wish to discuss it at the present time, we have more important things to do than argue over things that are already done with and can't be changed now that it has all happened. It is of no concern to me now, Kibitzer has already asked for forgiveness and I have granted him just that. Now please, no more of this bickering. This should be a time of celebration for the return of our fellow kinsman in blood, my blood, and your blood, too, Seraph. A fight amongst ourselves is death and disgrace in itself. We must stick together in the times to come, for all we may have is one another. We can trust no one, not even each other at times it seems," Raifen said.

"What of this curse now Kibitzer, please now, tell us more of this curse that banned you to the Marrow?" asked Seraph.

"I knew sooner or later I would have to restate the other prophecy, well, who knows there could be more, but this is the one I heard in town from one of the Nazracs:

> … another will come who lurks in the dark,
> he shall be the one who gives the mark,
> jealousy will lead him astray,
> and cursed he'll be, and soon won't stay,
> cast to the Marrow his soul shall be taken,
> brother in hand, a friend we'll see, or is he mistaken?
> to remain in the dungeons of Safewood,
> for reasons never clearly understood,
> a time shall arise when he may be set free,
> but how, he shall see.
> forever in the darkness he shall dwell,
> unless there is forgiveness to break the spell…

Raifen and Seraph just looked at each other, bewildered by this continuation of the prophecy. Who knew how many others there were?

"So, I was the one who came in the dark to try and kill Raifen. I was the one who was cursed to the Marrow, until the one in which I tried to kill came and forgave me of my sins. As you can see, this prophecy has been fulfilled. I am free and I have you to thank, Raifen."

"But Raifen why did you give me what I longed for all these years, instead of having revenge on me for trying to kill you when you were just a baby and gave you that scar?"

"Some things happen for a reason, some things happen because we choose for them to happen and some things happen because it's supposed to happen. I forgave you, Kibitzer, because I saw the suffering you had to go through while in the Marrow for eighteen years. I am one not to contain a grudge for long and also because you are my brother. Why would I leave my only brother in the Marrow? Why would I abandon him when he would not abandon me in the same circumstances? Would I have been no less as a tyrant to leave you there for your certain death? Would I have not been any better than you were when you tried to kill me? Would I not be any different from those awful creatures who serve Vlandrax Xen? Would I not be any different from the Bringer of Death himself?"

"I am not one of others. I do what I think is right and I do not follow other's wrongdoings only to be contained by the same sins of them who wish they had not committed. I am different from everyone else, Kibitzer, I have noticed that much on my own. I do not know how I was able to find the way out of the Marrow, only that I felt and asked for the woods to show it to me. I somehow was able to speak the same language as they who imprisoned you. The earth is a lot older and wiser than we think. It has lived and breathed all these many years, taken and given new life through evolution. For a brief moment I was encased in its infinite power. I could be mistaken, but it felt as if I were commanding it to show me, not asking. Not out of kindness did it show me but because it had to. As if I had control over it and could demand it whatever I wanted at whim.

"I do not know for sure how I was able to do it, but I am beginning to understand the secrets and ways of this gift I was foretold to have. I feel I only have to want something for it to happen. The control and power is something I can feel inside me. I find every time I am thinking of something I would like to happen, or willing it to come to pass, my scar burns and breathes off a reddish-green fume. Of late it seems to be a darker color; a color of no other. It seems overpowering. It is a tender and important subject to talk about and I, for one, do not yet understand it and can't speak of what it is until I know for sure. I believe it will tell me or I will finally understand when I need to understand."

Seraph and Kibitzer were dumbfounded by this sudden revelation of thoughts from Raifen. They believed him, yet they were frightened not only for him, but for themselves. Kibitzer and Seraph remained silent while Raifen thought and told his feelings of what was happening to him.

"I think we need to go see the Nazracs. They may have some answers that I need. We must hurry and find this storyteller, Clatistook. He can help us. If he can't, then we are on our own. Hurry and finish packing, I am going to go look for some more supplies in the forest. Try and find some answers from it as well. I'll be back around sundown. We'll leave in the morning."

MATTHEW THRUSH

With that last note, Raifen ran to the forest and disappeared into it, not to be seen until later that night. Meanwhile Seraph and Kibitzer put their faults and differences behind them and continued and worked together to gather the rest of the things they would need. Kibitzer lit a fire and Seraph got some biscuits and put some stew on in a small cooking pot for their little dinner to be.

A WILD HOUND CHASE

The morning was infused with sunlight like before. More clouds in the sky but nonetheless, still clear and shining brilliantly all the more. It was weird at first having Kibitzer along now, but exciting at the same time. Raifen would find himself ever so often staring at his brother; the hole inside of him seemed to have filled with a little something when Raifen had first found his brother. Now the emptiness didn't seem as oppressing as before.

"So, did you find out anything important on your little walk in the woods last night?" asked Kibitzer.

"Nothing really, just the same old whispering and murmurs flowing through and behind every tree and bush and rock, every surface. Nothing out of the ordinary." Except for the fact of trees speaking and me being able to hear them, he thought.

Kibitzer didn't seem satisfied by his brother's answer for seeing a look of remembrance shade across his face, then fade all the same, but decided not to push the subject any further at the time. Maybe later on he would ask him again, maybe in Petipala. Yes, he would wait until later. The wagon jostled along hitting and bumping into wondering roots and rocks. Bestrow, like usual, barked at nothingness. The silly dog was chasing what looked like a dirty squirrel, but looking closer Raifen suddenly realized it was no squirrel, it was a skunk.

"Bestrow, get away from that thing. Leave it alone."

Seraph and Kibitzer noticed what was happening as well and joined in with their own shouts of encouragement.

"Bestrow, you lousy mutt, you get over here right this instant. You hear me, get over here right now." Bestrow didn't seem to notice the shouting and he kept right on chasing the dirty squirrel.

"You're going to get sprayed you stupid dog. Get over here. Get away from that skunk."

"Leave it alone."

The skunk had enough of this annoyance, and it wound up on its front paws and displayed his weaponry warningly. Bestrow heeded not the warning and took the squirrel's sudden pause as an invitation to pounce on it. Oh did Bestrow ever get a shock at what came next. Boy that hound wound up on its hind legs and ran squealing back to un-welcoming wagon of Raifen, Seraph, and Kibitzer.

"Don't come whining to us, Bestrow, we told you to leave the poor old skunk alone. But did you listen, no, you had to find out the hard way all by yourself," replied Seraph with almost no pity in his voice.

"You'll be alright boy," a sympathetic Raifen encouraged.

"You old fool, I bet you learned your lesson not to go chasing weird looking squirrels from now on, huh?" adds Kibitzer joining in the mockery.

"The little weasel let him have it, huh boys?" stammered a laughing Seraph.

"Oh, he sure did," replied Kibitzer of who was now balling his eyes out with utmost laughter. All three had a good laugh for a while longer, all the while elaborating on the event more, making it even funnier than before. By the time they finally got to Petipala, they had the event all mixed up and changed, it was a whole different story, with nothing to do with Bestrow or the skunk.

Old Bestrow didn't take it all too well, he followed behind with his tail between his legs, not chasing a single thing the rest of the way to Petipala, but when there, that was a whole different story.

PART THREE: THE NAZRACS

The water splashed rapidly as the figure paddled his way across the roaring sea. Clearly his time was up. The figure looked over his shoulder several times on the way, often stopping in the rowing, soon to continue. He had completed his task the Atem des Todes had asked of him. The smell still lingered on his breath even now. The taste had been rewarding. And now, he was on his way to his next destination. The bodies had been arranged in an according fashion, each with things missing. Each with a certain amount of blood missing, taken from their veins: all of it. A container full of flasks sat huddled together in the back of the boat. He had sucked the blood from each victim slowly and skillfully, and then displaced it into glass apparatuses. The tubes rattled along in the boat as the figure switched from one side of the boat to the other, rowing determinedly. He knew they would not follow him. They could not follow him. He had made sure that there were no witnesses. Besides, if there were, their bodies, no doubt, had joined the carnage in the town center from the booby-trap he had left for any unwanted eyes, though in truth he really wanted others to find them and spread the news of his work. For that was the reason for leaving any signs of what had transpired anyway, right? The town of Kell had sufficed the figure for a time, but its resources had dwindled and now he sought a new home. Often he would leave his sparse apparatus of leaves and branches, his home, to go wandering off in the woods. One day, while scurrying about his normal transgressions, he came upon a shallow ravine. He had arched his head from one side to the next, examining the field of water. It had appeared at first that one could merely walk across the illusional plain of dirt, but it was not so. The figure had found out the only way he knew how to, by attempting it. He soon had found out that it was not land, merely covered with about a foot deep water, but an area of earth that sank when you stepped upon it. Soon he realized that the whole area, as far as he could see, was covered in the false liquid, filled with a muddy dirt substance. He had anxiously tested the new deformity. His fingers had probed the depths of its fiber, coating his hands and arms, knees and ankles, in a brown foam. The figure had walked around the whole spot, searching for a crossing. He had found none, except for one small patch of dry land that eavesdropped on the mud puddle and made itself somewhat as a safe haven if you were caught in the goo, an island of sorts, though pathetic. He had tied a ragged piece of root branch to the stump of a tree that loomed close by the abyss of tar. He tested the strength of his little makeshift rope with his weight, and then submerged himself in the slim. Instantly he could not move, let alone swim. His body felt as if it were being dragged down into the pit of the weird liquid. He fought to stay atop the surface but soon found that the struggle aided his sinking. He forced himself to relax and to focus. Remembering that he had tied himself to the root string, he slowly began maneuvering his body in the position facing the embankment of land. Patiently he began to draw himself nearer to the solid ground from where he had first jumped. Soon after he lay on the ground panting from the mere energy loss the effort had cost him. Apparently there was no way across the barren wasteland of liquid. *Quicksand.* He had thought long and hard on the closer encounter of death and that's what it had to be. There was no other explanation for the rapid undertow from the muddy water. Though it appeared to be solid, he knew it for what it was. *Quicksand.*

The figure was sweating freely now. The perspiration was easily finding the surface of his pores and soaking his outer skin layer with a damp cloth of liquid. As he peddled through the current of death, his mind trailed back to the first time he had come here. It was many weeks ago, but still the memory was sharp in his mind. It was officially the closest he had ever come to dying. He would remember that day as long as he lived. He grinned at the flailing hands of liquid dirt as it grabbed at the bottom of the boat. He was safe in the cockpit of his raft, as long as he remained there. It was a slow and tiresome task to sail across the river of dirt. But once he came to the other side, his heart leaped with anticipation and greed. A whole new land awaited his mastering hand and he would make it worth his time. He had been lucky ever stumbling across the entrance way to the river. He constantly told himself that it was not luck, but merely the destined fate that he should be the one who found it first. His feet touched the earth, after jumping out of his special harness of transportation, which had touched land. He dragged the boat up into the beach bed and tied it to a tree close by. The boat was light, much easier to use and turn than a normal boat. A smile crossed the figure's face again knowingly. His boat was not one of human hands. It was magic. The distant throb in his head assured him of his thoughts and the vibration on his leg agreed as well, reminding him of its presence on his belt. The Atem des Todes hung loosely from its appendage of leather. It had taught its predecessor the way of Cantor Ramo, the ability to make things float, even when floating was impossible. The blade had told him nothing was impossible through magic and that he would teach him all its secrets if he remained his humble servant. Yul had agreed, hungrily. He sought to gain as much knowledge of power as he could. People needed lessons to be taught to them and what better teacher to have than him, their own seed of greed to teach them. Yul peered out into the expanse of dry liquid and couldn't help suppress the pride he felt in attaining the impossible. The river of stone, as he called it, was impassable, another reason why he liked this place so much. If one tried to swim across, he would soon find his life's end. If one thought that crossing by boat was possible, he too would find he was wrong and be devoured by the river of stone, his pet. He later found out that he had discovered an island, one that was completely surrounded by the quicksand. For miles and miles it stretched at some places. The reality of foreclosure sought to overwhelm him, but it failed. Instead, he stretched out his arms in triumph. Victorious he was this day. Each and every day after would be filled with his mastering the art of dark magic. Soon he would be as powerful as his master. But he would not remain under its command forever. Once he attained as much from the blade of knowledge as could be offered, he would discard of its company.

And so it was, Yul lived on Rapture, his island he had discovered that sat off the coast of the Swift Islands, for many years. He journeyed far and wide in search of greater, more rewarding lands, but soon realized he had found the best. Its inaccessible location offered the greatest strategy against his enemies. All of which stood no chance against his growing power and lustful evil. He ravaged the towns along the coast of the Swift Islands, creating devastation for many. He was known around the islands and through the trade routes to distant main lands as a fierce and deadly foe. None dared go up against him. And soon, he chanced a leave from his home of Rapture. It had grown old. He had no more use for it and one day, mysteriously left. The Swift Islands remained unscathed after that.

There is a voice, quietly calling, whispering for anyone who would dare listen. Its voice is muffled by the tunnel walls. Its presence remained lost, untouched, unseen, unnoticed, for many years, until someone stumbled upon it by mistake. The blade had gotten its wish. Now it would have its revenge.

MEMORIES OF VLANDRAX XEN

BEAUTY IN THE HORIZON

The figure will choose his destiny, day by day. He shall walk alone at a time, but soon will find a friend. If he searches too hard, too deep, too often, he could be devastated by the lack of finding. But if he seeks too depravedly, he could be more encrypted. He must stay vigilant and awake. If he falters but a few strides in his walk, it could cost him. He can be seen walking around, within and around us, we people unaware of his presence. He will laugh at our feeble trials, failure after failure, to find him and bring him to justice. There shall be no such justice, unless it's his. There will be a time of heartache, a time for pain, a time for horror, and a time for love's death. This will come to pass. In the air shall drift his foul words, his hand biting at the sun's light, cursing it to darkness. And then he shall have his wish. Darkness will prevail and shower its seed of destruction upon the lands. It shall happen, there is no stopping what is to come. One will halt its coming, yes; waver his determination and weaken his discipline. She shall tempt him. And he shall listen.

FROM THE SCROLLS OF DERACY

Raifen," whispered Kibitzer. He nudged Raifen in the shoulder to wake him up. He did so slowly. Kibitzer bent down closer to his brother.

"Are you awake?" he asked.

"Yes," Raifen managed to mumble.

"Good. I don't have much time. I just wanted to say—"

Raifen cut him off. "What do you mean you don't have

much time?" he clearly was awake now. Kibitzer looked into the dark night, then back to his brother's face.

"I have something I need to take care of."

"Like what?" asked Raifen.

"I can't say. Just listen. I am leaving tonight, but I want you to meet me somewhere in a few days from now. Can you do that?" asked Kibitzer.

"Yes, but—"

"Good. In a few days from now meet me at a place called *Billowly Rise*. It's near the coast of the Tarklav Sea. If you aren't sure if you are close enough or not, look for the Plankta Forest. It's just before that. You understand?" asked Kibitzer.

"I think so," stammered Raifen. He clearly didn't understand why his brother was leaving and why he had to meet him somewhere he had no idea existed or was located for that matter.

"Why are you leaving?" Raifen asked again.

His brother frowned. "I can't tell you that right now. But one day I may fill you in on something. But not now. I got to go, now."

Kibitzer stood up and picked up the sack he had no doubt stacked with supplies and food from their supply. He strapped it around his waist and shoulder, and then turned to face his brother again.

"Remember," began Kibitzer, "meet me at the Billowly Rise. Don't forget. I will see you there. Goodbye, for now." Kibitzer didn't give Raifen time for rebuttal before he had vanished into the darkness. Raifen remained awake for several minutes pondering what his brother could possibly have to take care of so urgently that he must leave tonight, and then, asking him to meet him somewhere in private. Strange occurrences were afoot. Raifen would have to keep his eyes open to all possibilities. He fell asleep soon after, his mind closing itself from all the troubles of the world to gain some much needed rest.

When Raifen was awoken by a frantic Seraph, he explained Kibitzer's absence. It troubled Seraph to learn that he had left in the middle of the night on some mystery assignment, but he couldn't worry himself over such things. And so, he continued on their quest to the city of Blasa. They arrived shortly thereafter.

Blasa was a steaming cathedral of flaming rocks in the heat of the day. Rocks and dust scattered with every step the group of outsiders took. The city and houses were all bowered behind what looked to be a bulwark made of stone and metal. A high cliff rose up on the far side of the city, blocking any sort of attack it might have from the north. The city was a natural fortress of defense. Raifen and his uncle followed a few other wagons of people making their way toward this fortified sanctuary.

"It's huge," Raifen gasped.

"Quite so I would say. But don't get too caught up in its magnificence and forget your purpose of coming here" urged his uncle.

"You're right, but one can't help but to acknowledge its strength and solidness."

The city was swarming with early morning crowds of

women and children, hurrying each to try and be the first in line for a new special. A worn down looking sign with the name *Bradbucks* written on it seemed to be gathering the most crowds.

SOMETHING ISN'T RIGHT

Broman, the leader and scout of the group of wanderers, stopped and stooped down to study the tracks of their prey. Broman was no ordinary tracker, he was the best—a legend. Tale after tale explained that he could track anything, through any kind of weather, and no matter how old the tracks, he could get them.

"Boss man stops, take rest now we can," one of the men spoke.

"Yes, rest, Tildur. Lay down now," Tildur said reassuringly to himself.

"Shut up you fools." scowled Broman.

The men grumbled.

"There will be no rest and since your kind comrade here, Tildur, took the leisure of lying down without my say, we will track twice as hard and rest less."

Grunts and dismay were exchanged between the men, all eyes glared coldly at Tildur.

"Way to go Tildur, you forsaken piece of carcass," hissed one.

"You shut up, too, Bobler, you're in as much fault as Tildur here," shot Broman. "Let's go, dark should be coming soon, we don't want to lose time. We must make haste, we're about three days behind."

And they went, reluctantly, but sure. Darkness was indeed close and it caught up with the travelers and put them in a shroud of blackness. The moon offered little light and they were forced to track through blindness, their leader tirelessly tracking ahead. The men stumbled over many rocks and old roots that were long since dried up by the sun.

"How much farther do you think we have to go," asked Panitzer to a tired Tildur.

"No clue, but if we's keep this up much longer, I think I'm a-gonna collapse," replied Tildur.

"I wish the boss would stop for a sec so I could get my breath," a stammering Bobler remarked.

They went on a stumbling and complaining, everyone except the boss falling enough times to have dug a small crater in the ground. They could hardly keep their eyes open and Tildur was about to say something when he was cut short.

"Shh, quiet down you fools," insisted Broman. "Stay here and don't make a sound."

With no rebuttal they all gladly stopped, falling to the ground with a bang. Broman disappeared into the darkness leaving his comrades where they fell. He had heard something up ahead, something that shouldn't be there. The night was easing now into the deep slumber of rest. All nocturnal animals and insects had long since gone. Morning was easing toward the sky when Broman came staggering out of the dark.

"Get your things together, now!"

For just a glimpse Tildur thought he had seen the suggestion of panic in Broman's eyes. It was dark, he couldn't be sure what he saw, but for one thing something had to be wrong for Broman to be shouting for them to get moving. Tildur and the others argued not and had no grunting

MATTHEW THRUSH

disapprovals for they all knew this was out of character for Broman to get all jumpy.

"What do you think it is Tildur?" asked a nervous Bobler.

"Not sure, but if it upsets the boss like this, I don't want to be the one to find out," replied Tildur.

SOFAL

The creature was close, much closer than its prey thought, much nearer than their sweetest hopes. Like them it had tracked what it was after. It tracked the same thing, the same being, and the same destiny. Fate often came to its wielder, the slothticker. An ugly, twisted, muscle deformed being with dangling crusted hair pieces covering his entire body. It wore a hooded cloak about itself, to not draw attention, and most of all to hide its appearance. The slothticker knew how to stay in the shadows, the darkness somewhat conformed to his presence and made him one with the surroundings. He was a good tracker at one time, long, long ago when he was still classified as human, as a creature of the lifecycle, but now that had all changed. He no longer was the pure hearted boy of ten years old like before, nor the loving father of three, two boys and a girl. He no longer was the caring and good looking husband that so much was adored by his beautiful wife. No, none of these things were and never will be for that matter. He was transformed, chosen I guess it could be said, by the fate that binds him this day. The curse that finds us all, found him sooner.

Death.

It was quite a good time ago when it happened. It was a normal day like the rest, nothing out of the ordinary, nothing out of place, nothing strange, nothing new, except what he was to find. The thing that destined him to whom and what he became comes down to this one thing, this one

MATTHEW THRUSH

moment, this one life-altering desire. Upon walking into his well-built house of fine woods and metals he found them there all bloodied and torn, shredded of all life, his lovely wife, his two boys, and his precious baby girl. All of them spread out on the floor. Sofal, for he did have a true name at one time, could contain himself no longer.

He combusted with a slurring wind of insanity, madness so deep and uncontrolled, that it consumed him from body to soul. His heart was soaked clean with blackness, converted to wickedness so evil that darkness failed to keep it contained. He was filled with a devouring hatred. It came from deep and locked up crevices in his soul where he kept all his feelings, his deepest and darkest secrets. He fed off them. He took life from all those evil thoughts and gave himself power. Vengeance would come one day. He vowed his life to it. Everything, every person he killed, was a piece of himself being taken back. Now that he was what he had become, there was no turning back. The sloth crouched to the damp ground and searched for freshly made tracks. It smelled for the scent it was after: victims. There was not much brush or trees around but a few misshapen furs and bushes left to dry out in the sun. The dirt was hard and thickly laid with rocks, making it difficult for the sloth. The use of its magic though did give an edge. The sloth began to sway from side to side, eyes closed, mind stretching wide with the magic it contained. For quite some time the sloth maintained this stance. The sun was easing gently to the east casting a moist blanket of colors of bright yellow and orange when the sloth's eyes shot wide open. It started at once.

PAST BECOMES PRESENT

Raifen was beginning to tire of all the walking they had done since leaving the dark forest and he had to rest.

"Uncle, I got to stop."

His uncle looked up at his nephew's worn face and saw his own face reflected there. He too was exhausted and utterly spent from the piercing heat of this land. It was much warmer in these parts, with less green and lush countryside's filled with streams and wild trees. Yes, this was a desert land, the Blasandi Desert it was called, named after the great king Blasad who traveled across the lands and here where he had to lay to rest under the steaming sun in a small pile of evergreens, or at least that's what he thought they were. Seraph thought back on the stories he had been told as a boy, the jokes and tales of the great King Blasad coming back from his past memories. The king had traveled with a mighty army, but now was reduced to about eleven others, twelve counting himself though he didn't know how much longer he would last or his companions for that matter. They were strong and dependable men. Trustworthy and courageous when their arm was needed: eight hardy men, two wary dwarfs, and a kin of the elves. The elf was the main reason they had come to the land. He claimed that this was a lost land to his people and wished to come and behold where his ancestors had once lived. He told of how the gods would come once a year to a race that was held in the desert, the mighty Dicatron, it was called.

Those times the land was filled with fields of grass and layered with trees of all sorts. This was a beautiful land long ago. But one day, the day of the race when the gods came down and roamed the streets with the townspeople, there was a disaster. The plague came quickly, a sudden mirror effect of what could happen, and did happen to the land. There was a thief named Heddrox who was widely known for his thievery and deceit. He was banished from the land but sneaked back into the gates of the city each time he was thrown out. It was one too many people would say. Heddrox had only a few days earlier been dropped off at the stream of Gaylasakai, not ten miles from the town.

"Don't come back again, Heddrox," guards said, "or next time it won't be so pleasant of a stay."

They all laughed and bullied Heddrox and beat him up for a matter of fact. Heddrox was bleeding from all over. From his mouth, his nose, his ears, and eyes, and even most likely in places he didn't know about. Heddrox was in pretty bad shape and almost died, but a woman's grace saved him. Essabella, oh sweet Essabella. The goddess of right and peace. She saw what the men had done to him and hated them for it. A god's hate is a powerful thing. She bent down close to Heddrox's weak body. The fresh grass now soaked in his own blood. The air came in rasps each time Heddrox tried to breathe, and each time he did a little bit of blood was sucked into his lungs as well. Heddrox didn't have much time to live—only a few hours at most.

"Heddrox," Essabella spoke, her voice a melody of dreams catching Heddrox immediately.

"Errr, who is there, ugh," Heddrox asked, coughing with the trouble of speaking.

"It is I."

Heddrox managed to turn his head to the left just enough to see the speaker's face. Through a swollen eye he looked up.

"Essabella?"

The strength came back to him now with the kindness he saw in her face, the beauty and power in those eyes.

He knew who she was. Everyone did. She was the daughter of the mightiest god known to man, Wrenthaos. He was the ruler of all the gods and controller of all the lands. He was feared by all. It was rumored that when he spoke his voice could be heard for miles and when he walked the earth would shake like thunder. He had eyes that could pierce you and make you feel exposed completely. This was the daughter of the mighty god.

"I have been watching you Heddrox."

"You-u hav-ve?" he stuttered.

"Yes I have. I find you intriguing, young Heddrox. I also saw the things that you have done, and also what others have done to you as well."

Heddrox didn't say anything. He didn't know what to say. Why would Essabella be watching him? In truth, he not only was curious, but also terrified.

"I know you," she said.

Heddrox was speechless no longer.

"How is that? I have secrets."

"True, but doesn't everyone?"

The smile that she had was not one of mockery, but rather sincerity.

"I know more than you think I do, Heddrox. Much more than you expect."

Heddrox just continued to look at her. The thoughts of why she was here talking with him, a forsaken meeting that was punishable by death.

"I have come to show you something Heddrox."

She placed her hand upon his chest and closed her eyes. Heddrox could hear her soft breathing as her chest rose and fell. Nothing happened at first. Heddrox didn't know what to think, he thought that she was just being kind in touching an unworthy soul to grant him courage through his experience. Oh how wrong he was to think that was all she was capable of and willing to do. The thrumming began softly at first, but quickly enhanced in pressure. Heddrox saw the bluish mist coming from her hand. The hues mixed with one another and formed like tentacles, reaching out for him, absorbing themselves in his body. Heddrox's body began to shake with compulsions as the mist seeped into his bloodstream bringing an overwhelming coldness to his body.

The last thing he remembered was seeing Essabella whipping her head back all of a sudden and screaming a horrifying scream filled with bright white fumes, which blanketed around him and began to somewhat suffocate him. Then everything went black.

AGREED

Seraph came to the end of his revelations and agreed.

"We'll find a cheap place to stay for the night."

That was all he said for that's all his strength would allow. The horses came to a halt at a gated inn. People of both genders and all races could be seen. There was a bar in the inn and Raifen and Seraph both sat down to have a refreshing drink. Many people were sitting all around them, some talking in loud, obnoxious tones, and others in hushed ones.

Raifen and Seraph tried to remain licit. They were foreigners in a way and sense and they wished not to be given too much unnecessary attention at the moment. They would rather be in and out of this place without a hint of discordance. They would get neither of their wishes as they would find out.

UNKNOWING WAKE

H eddrox slowly opened his eyes. His whole body ached from some unimaginable pain or suffering, yet he didn't remember what exactly happened to him. He managed to sit up in his cushioned bed and get a look around in the small, enclosed shack, or whatever the place was. His feet touched the chilly ground causing him to jump back in surprise. Chilled shivers raked up and down his body, pulsating his veins with an unneeded stress. He narrowed his eyes and peered around his captivity. The room was about ten feet by ten feet, a large room in commoner standards.

There was a weird presence about the room that made Heddrox uneasy. There seemed to be some evil force about the place, or some kind of spirited presence, or life force that dwelled here, within these solid walls. Something wasn't right here. He could feel it in his bones. His heart throbbed and ached, urging him that his suspicions were correct and that he should get out of there, and fast, before it was too late.

"I shouldn't be here," whispered Heddrox to himself as he continued to analyze his small sanctuary. He was soon to find out how right he was.

New Understanding

hat have ya," asked an awkward looking man.

Seraph looked at Raifen, then back at the ghastly appearance of the person talking to them. To think he could be human was a feat itself. He looked to be some four feet tall. No taller than the bar table itself, his eyes barely reached over the top. He looked dwarfish, but had the appearance of some kind of small Rangor. His skin was all dirty and darkened from the sun. His nose was bent to one side and his chin was crunched up. His auburn hair hung down his face, blotting out his left eye from view. He was apposing in appearance.

"Solid as stone," the dwarves said. "You work in the mines, the mines work on you."

"Anything," Seraph gasped. The heat had really gotten to his bones today. He felt old indeed.

"Anything? Huh, you musts be wantin' somethin'," snarled the bartender. "You's walks in here place and asks for anything, bah. I've be layin' an egg before I'ze believe ya ta be wantin' just that."

The bartender began to get moodier by the second. He slammed his fist on the table.

"Whats have ya?" he demanded.

Seraph was hesitant to answer and that really got the bartender going.

"I'ze asks ya a question and I'ze expects a answer."

"What do you have?" Seraph finally asked.

MATTHEW THRUSH

The bartender's face turned deep scarlet. His eyes bulged out of their sockets. Sweat dripped down his face, mixing with the drool now seeping through the crevice between his teeth falling down his chin and onto the table. His body tensed up and it appeared he was going to explode. But right when it looked as if he were going to burst, a woman quickly came and grabbed him by the arm and slapped him on the cheek.

"Shame on you, Charles," said the woman. "Treating the customers like this. Now go tend to some tables around here, I'll take it from here."

Charles mumbled something under his breath and moped across the room and began gathering dishes. He glared at them and hissed as he went about.

"Don't mind him, he's just a little defensive against strangers. My name's Lousie, how can I be of service to you fellows today?"

Raifen couldn't help but notice this woman had a seductive kind of beauty about her. Maybe it was the way she held herself, shoulders straight, eyes forward, seemingly as if she were of royal heritage or something. Her eyes were captivating as well. His eyes locked with hers for a second and then he came back from his inner glories when she joined him in his little game of eye tag. He turned in embarrassment, his cheeks a little pink. There was a period of awkward silence, neither Seraph, Raifen, or the woman said anything. Raifen took this opportunity to speak up.

"Well, we've come a long way and we're real beat from the sun. If it's not too much trouble, we would like something cool to drink and a comfortable place to stay."

"I can do that for ya."

"Thanks." As she went about making them drinks, she didn't hesitate to probe them with questions. It wasn't every day you had travelers come into your bar. She was eager to know why they were here. They didn't look like the sort of people who would be traveling with a caravan or on their own. Nope. There was something mysterious about these two and she was going to find out what.

"What brings you two fellows to Petipala this time of year?" she asked, sending the first and direct question full blow, not holding anything back.

"Business," Seraph quickly replied.

"What kind of business?" she asked. She would stop every now and again to look back over her shoulder from tending another customer to hear their reply.

"We're here looking for someone."

Lousie frowned. It wasn't anything new for people coming in looking for someone. People always had someone they were trying to get back at for a mishap. And all else that was needed. The questions were boundless. She thought nothing different about these two. But she was wrong.

"He is a storyteller," continued Seraph, drawing back Lousie's attention immediately, though she tried to mask her curiosity and shock. It was too late; Seraph had seen the look.

"You ever heard of him?" he asked quizzically.

A hush filled the room. Everyone looked over at Seraph and Raifen. No one said a word. Lousie's face was pale and stricken with despair. Her eyes seemed to bulge a little, making her look a little ghostlike. She didn't answer. Lousie went to the cupboard as if she was looking for something. She came back with two cups of ale and then left. Raifen and Seraph were aghast. A few feet shuffled on the floor and Raifen turned to see some of the customers leaving the bar.

"Did I say something wrong?" Seraph asked, speaking his thoughts more to himself than to anyone else. The remainder of the bar looked one last time at Seraph and Raifen then went back to what they were doing. The noise quickly returned and you could hear the sound of rash arguments taking place amongst the men. One man caught Raifen's eye though. He stayed in the shadows, keeping from the main crowds, not making a move to draw attention to himself. A dark hood covered his face from the light. A faint red glow lazed out from the cloak every so often, the remnants of smoke drifting up to the ceiling. There was something strange about this guy. Unusual. Something that spoke to his heart he should stay away from the hooded man. There was something mysterious about the man's presence that gave Raifen a weird feeling in his gut. He watched the figure and it watched him back. After a few seconds went by, Raifen shook the matter aside and quickly consumed his drink. The figure in the corner was still there. Watching. Lousie came back later and told them where they would be staying for the night. She gave Seraph a key to room four. And then, just as before, disappeared.

The night was cool, much cooler than earlier, but still there was a dryness about it that kept a person on the uncomfortable side. The moon was shining brightly in the dark sky. It cast its lit shadow on the surrounding buildings bringing a dim light to the streets. Its presence gave off an eerie feeling to the strangers of these parts. This light was the source of direction for Raifen and Seraph, as they groped about in the darkness trying to find their room. Strange people hung around in corners of the streets and in the alleys. They looked up at Raifen and Seraph as they made their way along the building.

"Where is the dang room?" growled Seraph. He was beginning to get a little uneasy with all these people hanging around. All he wanted was to find their room, be out of the streets, and get some much needed rest. How much was that asking? Finally, after much searching, they came to their room. A rusty, almost unhinged, *four* hung limply on the door. It appeared no one had inhabited the room for some time. Seraph opened it up and they entered. They were instantly absorbed in darkness, impenetrable and crippling. Raifen felt uneasy. A faint light ignited a few feet away and he could see the illumination of lines of age in Seraph's face. Seraph lit a candle and the room slowly came into focus. The space was cramped, hardly much room to maneuver around. One small bed stood at the far end, in a corner. Like the room, it too was worn, and a sign of brokenness was written all over it. A single sheet lay on it, and a dirty one at that. There was hardly any furniture: a small table, two crooked chairs, and a closet. Raifen could only guess what lay in there.

"Well, home sweet home," stammered Seraph, with a far from satisfying look on his face. Raifen grinned.

"As close as we are gonna get for awhile." They both had a laugh and it somewhat relaxed them, though the reality of that statement shook Raifen to the core.

"You go ahead and sleep on the bed, Uncle. I'll go ahead and make up a bed on the floor," stated Raifen.

Seraph was too tired to argue, so after a few unsure glances and nods Raifen's way, he agreed.

"Okay."

Raifen found a ragged broom in the closet and tried to sweep some of the filth and grim away from his uncle's sleeping quarters and away from the spot on the floor that he had picked as a winner. He got some blankets out of his loin sack and tossed one to Seraph. Seraph nodded in thanks and plopped down on the bed. Raifen put his bag on the floor and laid a blanket over it. After deciding that it would suffice, he collapsed as well. He was exhausted from the day's experiences. He lay there staring up at the ceiling. The light of the candle shot shadows on the ceiling and the walls, little dark spots playing games with their minds.

"Goodnight, Uncle."

"Night."

Raifen closed his eyes, begging sleep to take him. Hoping to be restored and rested for the next day.

Under the dim lamppost outside Raifen and Seraph's room, the man was crouched in the shadows. He would wait a little longer to make sure they were down for the night, then make his move. He would not rush things. That was the worst thing you could do. He would be patient. Patience was necessary in his field of work.

He was a tracker and one of the best, but not only that, he was an assassin, unnaturally skilled in his position. He had been following their trail for days now waiting for them to stop. His mind and training told him to wait and be silent, but his heart spoke a different tune. Hatred. His heart was consumed by it. If he were not careful it would take hold of him again. He could not let that happen, at least not yet. My time would come he would tell himself over and over again, reassuring his madness. His skilled fingers edged the hilt of his dagger in anticipation. While hidden in the dark, a lone figure came hobbling along on a cane towards room number 4. The one the figure was watching. The figure sank back deeper into the shadows. He would wait. Yes. For now, he would wait.

Raifen was the first to wake up, jumping straight up off the floor. Seraph, too, was clawing his way out from under the covers on the third knock.

"What in God's name!"

Raifen went over to the window, which stood two feet from the door.

Who could be knocking on our door at this hour of the night, he thought to himself. A bent over figure loomed just out of sight in the overhanging shadows of the lamp light. Seraph was now fully awake, standing at the door. He looked over at Raifen and nodded his head. Raifen understood.

"Who is it?" asked Seraph.

No answer.

"Who's there?" asked Seraph more sternly.

They could hear a clanking of metal on the brick sidewalk. The person was moving around.

"What do you want?" Seraph asked, deciding to get to the bottom of this disturbance. He had just been settling in a deep sleep when he was awakened by the banging on the door.

A gurgling sound was now coming from the other side of the door, a rustling of papers and then a soft humming. Right when Raifen and Seraph realized it was some kind of chanting it was too late. The door flew right into Seraph slamming him against the wall. There was the smell of burning wood. Clear smoke steamed in the opening where the door had once been. The figure walked in. Raifen went rigid. The man was old extremely old, from the look of it. Gray hair covered the majority of his face allowing only for his solemn nose and the long crusted beard on his chin to stand out. He wore a brown cloak and around that he had strapped some kind of religious symbol. Raifen could tell that it was a disguise, but for what reason it held, he did not yet know.

"Who are you?" asked Raifen.

The man didn't answer. He just looked from Raifen to Seraph and then back to where he had come from.

"Come with me." he said.

Raifen and Seraph didn't move. The man turned and saw that they weren't following.

"There's not much time. Come now!"

No movement.

"You're in danger," the man shouted. "We haven't much time, come now. Hurry!"

Raifen didn't budge. "Who are you?"

"A friend. Now come, please." The man started to leave again. He stuck his head back in the opening and spoke, one word, *clayershoia*, meaning believe and you shall see.

Raifen was moving then, Seraph right behind him. The man walked hurriedly, his cane clanking noisily on the road. He hobbled in a strange off-balanced kind of rhythm. They went around a corner, down an alley, then around another corner. They went like this for what seemed like forever, up and down winding streets. Raifen was instantly lost. He found himself regretting he ever left the room, let alone with a mysterious man who knew how to speak *scaomagea*. He knew of only two people who could speak it—himself and his mother. His mother was dead so that only left him and he knew he had never told anyone of it. It was the language his mother always used to sing to him in his dreams. She used to always say one word to him all the time. This word was one of the main things he remembered of his mother. Clayershoia. Believe and you shall see. He always knew there was something more about it, but never knew what it was. For this stranger to be speaking it was mystifying.

"Just a little farther, we're almost there," encouraged the ghost.

Raifen had decided that he had to be some ghost sent from another realm for a reason, a purpose. Raifen was going to find out what that reason was, no matter what it took. The ghost took them around one last bend and then stopped. Raifen barely had time to keep from running into him he had stopped so abruptly. Raifen, a little

MATTHEW THRUSH

shaken up from the unexpected halt, now began to relax and looked around at where they had come. They were in a clearing of some sort. Dark black trees circled them from all directions. The moon had made its way on the other side of the trees, causing it to be even darker now. It was unnaturally quiet here. Too quiet for Raifen's liking. The old man walked over to the middle of the clearing and bent down. He played with the dirt in his hands, fingering a symbol on the ground. Raifen couldn't see what he was writing from where he stood so he made for a closer look. The man seeming to know his thoughts held out his other hand, keeping him where he was.

"Just a little longer." he whispered. "It's almost done."

A few more seconds passed and then the man stumbled to his feet. He walked over to where Raifen and Seraph were standing.

"Watch," he said. "Just watch real close."

Raifen looked. He didn't see anything out of the ordinary. The only thing he saw was...

What? How could that be? That's strange, he thought to himself.

The ground where the old man had just been began swirling. Twisting and turning in one small circle. A light was shooting out from the center of this whirlpool of rock. It seeped out onto the spinning dirt and began to mix with it, changing colors. It went from white to a deep scarlet, then to a lighter bluish hue and to a fiery red and green. It continued to change different hues and finally rested to a smooth purple. The man walked over and peered into the looming blackness of the abyss. He glanced over his shoulder then disappeared down the hole. Raifen and Seraph didn't know what to think. They were both frozen in place at the mere happenings of the night and this strange old man who said he was a friend. And now, the image of him jumping down a pit that had just sprung up out of the ground, it was madness.

"Come on down," the man's voice echoed out of the hole. "You'll find it's quite safe."

Raifen edged toward the hole. He peered through the dimness of the moon down the opening. The light shone through just a little, some three feet at the most. He couldn't see much and wondered where the man had gone. He quickly found out when a firm hand grabbed him and tugged him down. He felt like he were falling forever. But in reality he had only been falling for about half a second before hitting solid but soft ground. He landed on some kind of straw platform. It seemed to have been thrown there roughly, in not any order. Raifen looked up to see his uncle clawing his hands up toward the sky as he too fell down crashing next to him. He got up and brushed the dirt off his clothes. The dust floated in their nostrils making them cough. Raifen peered through the mist and saw a flickering light just off to the side. It illuminated the outline of some small tunnel that ran underneath the earth. A torch sprung to life three feet from where Raifen was standing. Through the light that it gave he could see the old man's face, the crisp beard, and the smile that was abroad it.

"Follow me, please," he spoke. Then he turned around and headed through the tunnel. Raifen and Seraph followed him.

"I hope this guy is really a friend," said Raifen with a nervous look on his face.

Seraph just nodded. The tunnel was cramped. Letting only someone who was about five feet tall walk through it unhinged, Raifen and Seraph both had to squat down not to hit their heads on the ceiling and any dangling roots from above. The tunnel winded sideways sometimes, but mainly it seemed to stay straight. Raifen and Seraph followed the torch's light flashing off the tunnel walls. The old man was ahead of them now and the light was all that kept them from losing him completely and becoming utterly lost. They sure didn't want that to happen down here in the dark, underneath the ground, their screams being muted by the surrounding dirt. Raifen had a strange feeling he was being buried alive. It kept him on the jittery side. The tunnel rounded another bend and then opened abruptly into a small chasm in the rock. It was a room of some sort. Candles were lit all over the sides of the walls. There was a small cot a few feet away, a desk with some books, and a few chairs leaning against the wall. The old man was making his way around the room lighting candles adding light to the place. The torch was planted in a stake on the wall shining light down another tunnel. Raifen had no intentions yet to find out where it led. Raifen and Seraph huddled next to each other by the opening, looking unsure of what to do.

"Come sit down, please make yourselves at home," the old man said without looking over his shoulder. He motioned to the chairs against the wall in the far corner. Seraph headed for them. Raifen stayed where he was.

"Is this where you live?" he asked.

The old man kept at what he was doing not making any expressions as to hearing Raifen's words. Raifen waited. Seraph now came back and handed Raifen a chair. They both sat down, slumping instantly. They both relaxed a bit now and watched the old man for awhile. The old man didn't seem to notice and finished lighting the last of the candles. He set it down and turned to face them. His face was stern when he turned to them. It caught Raifen off guard and the feeling of uneasiness crept back into his bones.

"Yes, this is my home. Well, for now at least. It does the job."

There was an awkward silence. The man sighed and ran his hand through his beard. He went and propped himself on a chair as well and sat down a few feet from Raifen and Seraph. He sighed again.

"Do you know who I am?" he asked. "Do you know why I have come to you, why I have brought you to this place?"

No answer. Raifen and Seraph just watched.

"My name is Clatistook. I am a foreteller of futures, myths, fables, and dreams. I have seen something tonight in a dream that frightened me." He paused. "You are in danger."

"What kind of danger?" asked Raifen.

Clatistook hesitated.

"A deadly and dangerous danger if you are not careful. I have seen what could happen."

He sunk his head toward his chest. Breathing in slow

and deep breaths. Trying to get his nerves together for what he was about to tell Raifen.

Seraph saw the terror in Clatistook's eyes.

"What's wrong?" he asked. "Who or *what* is after us?"

"An evil greater than these lands have seen for centuries. An evil that has no compassion. An evil consumed by hatred."

He fell silent again. "He is called the sloth. He is an assassin who has been consumed by hatred and vengeance. He blames everyone and everything for his family's deaths. He does the Bringer of Death's work. He was assigned to kill you. His task was soon to be finished, too, but I showed up and caused him to wait. He is anxious for your death; he gains power when he kills. He takes part of that person with him and it gives him new strength." He stopped to allow this to soak in. "I came to you for a reason. I know who you are. I know of the tales that were told by the Nazracs years ago. I know your blood line and where it flows. I know what you are supposed to do to change the outcome that has already been set."

Raifen was excited now. This was the reason for him going to Blasa. He was about to find out what his purpose was.

"All these things I will tell you, in time. But now is not the time or place to share it. There are evil spirits lurking around. Prying in on conversations. Taking in as much information so that when they return to their lord, he will be pleased with their work."

"Can you tell me where I can find the Nazracs?" Raifen asked.

"Sure I can. But why?" The old man looked puzzled.

"I need to go there. I need to find out who I am," Raifen said, looking flustered.

"I know where they reside, yes. I will not tell you though."

"But why not?" asked a curious Raifen.

Clatistook seemed to have expected this and quickly answered, "Because I'm going with you."

He said it in a way that left no room for rebuttal.

"Now, if I were you I would get some rest. We leave tomorrow. The sooner the better."

Raifen was a little upset about leaving so soon, but he didn't say anything. Besides, sleep sounded so good right now, he didn't want to ruin it with an argument.

The last thing Raifen had heard was Clatistook telling his uncle: "These lands are very dangerous. It would be wise if we left tonight, but it's better to travel when you are well rested. I can only allow for you to rest one night, that is all." Seraph had been quiet the whole time. Raifen was wondering why and when the darkness took him.

Wake up. Wake up. It's time to go, hurry," a worried Clatistook whispered. Raifen was just having a dream about being in the mountains with his mother. She was all dressed in white linen clothing and he was just wearing a plain shirt and some pants. He was all muddy from having run from the house to see her. He had heard her calling his name in the scaomagea language. The language he and his mother spoke had a secret power that only they knew. It allowed them to do certain things that normal ordinary people could not do. He had taken her hand and they were walking through the woods in the Amaranth, the place of his mother's residing when he had heard his name being called. Someone was telling him to wake up. He didn't understand why someone was saying wake up when he was awake. He had looked to his mother for understanding and she had just smiled. *Go Raifen. I will meet with you again, but now you must go. Hurry, Raifen, something is wrong, you must be quick.* That was the last thing he remembered from his dream when he woke up. Clatistook was whispering in his ear, nudging him gently but firmly. When he had seen that Raifen was awake he left to go finish some other business. Raifen blinked his eyes trying to get a better focus on his surroundings. The room was still dark. A faint light was shining from a small candle next to where Clatistook was moving about. He seemed in a hurry for some reason.

"What time is it?" asked a tired Raifen. He wasn't sure how long he had been asleep but it sure felt like it wasn't long. His muscles were still cramped and tired from the long journey the day before. All of the realities of his journey were quite tiresome.

"It's still late in the night," Clatistook quickly stated. "You have only been asleep for a few hours. I'm sorry I woke you but we must go."

Raifen frowned. "Go? Why?"

"Not the time, not the place, we must leave now. Someone has found my lair. How they found it is beyond my knowledge right now, but it's bad news. We must leave before they find this room and all of us in it." Raifen looked around the room for his uncle and any signs of someone coming in through the tunnel. He saw none. Seraph was packing the things just as fast, if not faster, than Clatistook. He looked frightened. His pale eyes looked over to Raifen and seemed to say *sorry*. Raifen knew it wasn't Seraph's fault they had to leave so soon but he wished he could do something about this person who was following them. He sat there for a few moments pondering his options. He finally decided on it. He stood up, went to the tunnel entrance and began to walk. Seraph saw him and came running over to stop him. He grabbed Raifen's arm and tugged much harder than Raifen would have liked.

"Where are you going?" stammered Seraph.

"There is something I must do first. I'll catch up to you."

"You can't leave, there's a man coming this way. He must not see you."

"Uncle, I must do this, for all of our sakes. Trust me. I know what I must do. I'll meet you on the other side of that tunnel over there." He pointed over to where the other tunnel he had seen earlier started. "You and Clatistook go through there, I'm sure it's a way out. Stay with Clatistook, he knows the way."

"How do you know this?" asked a quite confused Seraph.

Raifen sighed and shrugged his shoulders. "I just do." Without any other further explanation he left. He had looked back once since and was now regretting his decision to leave. He knew what he must do, but he wasn't so sure it was a good idea. He had come about three hundred feet into the tunnel and still there was no sign of the intruder.

He was running now instead of a brisk walk. But he stopped suddenly when he heard someone else's approach. The other did the same as well, obviously hearing his coming, too. There he sat, in the darkness of the tunnel. Dust from his footsteps choking him and it was all he could do to not sneeze. A minute had passed and still no sign of this man had shown. Raifen was getting nervous. He was about to move when he heard a tiny bristle of dirt being crushed under a silent, but powerful, foot right next to him. His body jerked all at once. Raifen started to run. The man was on him instantly. Raifen felt a piercing pain run through his shoulder as he was lunged into the ground, slamming hard in the solid dirt. Dust flew in his mouth and he coughed. Powerful hands groped for footholds on his clothing, inching closer to his throat each passing second.

The killer could smell the taste of death in his mouth. The hatred had come all at once while he was in the bushes. He couldn't hold it back and had followed his prey to their secret hiding place. In truth, he was in awe at how skilled it was hidden. It had taken him all of three hours to locate it. But when he did, he had tracked them all the way through the tunnels. He knew he was getting close when the smell had suddenly become more intense. He could sense something near, something or someone giving off fumes of frightfulness. He had skillfully sneaked to the person hiding in the corner of the tunnel. He had heard the person's footsteps a few moments before and had also heard the sudden depletion of them as well. The sloth knew he had heard someone coming too, but he was better. And the sloth knew it. Now here he was rolling around on the ground with his victim. He could feel life seeping away from his prey's body.

Raifen was gasping for breath. The killer was choking him. He was pinned against the side of the tunnel and couldn't move. He felt his life leaving him. He pushed to stay awake but it was too strong. He could feel consciousness fading away. His body was relaxing now and he ushered it on. He could hear his killer's voice echoing in his ears.

"Ahhh, yes, I can feel it. Come to me," and then a shrill laugh.

Raifen closed his eyes and welcomed the calm and the blackness that filled his vision. He let go.

The man was breathing harder now, with expectancy. He could feel the body beneath his hands going rigid, the first sign of its life coming to an end. He squeezed harder and tightened his grip on his victim's neck. The pulse was slowing—beating ever so often and barely audible. The sloth was anxious now. He had been waiting for this moment for a long time. He had anticipated the way it would feel to gain more energy through the death of yet another victim. A victim that his master had said would be a great victory. The creature beneath his hands felt so weak and vulnerable. How could this pathetic being be so important to his master? What was so frightening about this boy? How was he a threat to Vlandrax Xen's plans of conquering the lands? What was so … He didn't get the chance to finish the rest of his contemplation.

MATTHEW THRUSH

The peace was sinking in now. Raifen could feel it. He welcomed the feeling of letting go and finally being set free. His body felt a calmness that it had not seen for a long time. The blackness of his thoughts and vision were getting darker.

But Raifen was not scared. Raifen was about to enter another level of darkness when he heard his mother's voice speaking to him. It caught him off guard. Why was his mother here too? How had she found him? He focused in on her voice and listened to her words.

"Ble gottsha bea leakaoh, enamana bushoola keekala-baa." *Come back my son. You are stronger than this.*

Something inside of Raifen sprung to life then. He could feel the energy running through his veins, a new source of power awakening from its deep slumber. He listened to his mother's voice still, gaining courage and strength from each passing word.

"Keekaloa badaclokishea abadose iecha. Loucaozaa balakeeloa reloshaoe. Keekaloa." *Fight back, you have the power. Resist the calling and take command. Fight back.*

Raifen understood. He knew what he had to do. He could feel the power welling up inside his body, flowing from the crevice of his soul to the heart and fleeing to his body and fingers, ushering a command of power that nothing could resist.

His eyes shot open. It startled the sloth. It was not expecting this to happen. It had felt its prey's pulse slowing and almost completely gone. It had been getting anxious and greedy for its kill. The smile on its face had vanished when the body under its palms came to life. The sloth became nervous and began to squeeze harder around the neck of its victim. There was a heat unlike anything it had ever felt before, even hotter than the fires that had burned its skin when it ran into the burning house to save its family. Deadlier than the hatred that had consumed its body and formed it into something demonic—into a lonesome beast, a creature. The sloth tried to pull away from its victim, but its hands were held firm. The sloth screeched in pain. It could feel its hands melting.

The sloth heard some kind of guttural sound coming from the victim's mouth. It didn't seem like any language it had ever heard. It sounded like gibberish and croaking sounds. Over and over again it echoed from its prey's mouth. The sound of it made its body quiver. Something the sloth hadn't done for a long time. The voice frightened the sloth and it jumped back from the victim on the floor. It could feel his body shaking now, an uncontrollable seizure taking hold of it. It could feel itself becoming paralyzed and unable to move its legs to run away. It sat in utter horror at the image of its powerless prey lying on the verge of death to a shimmering light blinding it. The colors were clear and beautiful. Something that was extremely painful for the sloth to behold. The sloth covered its face with its arms, but the light shown through still. It couldn't take it any longer. It had to escape and flee this menace, *this demon.*

The sloth ran through the tunnel back the way it had come, stumbling over its feet and tripping, knocking its face a few times into the rock. Fresh blood was dripping from its nose. It felt its lip swelling to double its normal shape. Its right arm was aching tremendously. It crashed through the opening in the earth that it had stumbled upon and fell into the bushes. The sloth slumped against a tree to catch its breath. Its arm was broken, it knew that much. The bone was protruding from the skin. It had to get away; it needed to find its master. He would know what to do. He must know what to do. The sloth began running again, more urgently now. The sloth fell again and this time did not get up for awhile. It lay sprawled out on the ground clenching its right arm. Oh, how it hurt. It had been so long since the sloth could feel anything. The pain was too much. It was on the verge of blacking out but it had to keep going. It struggled to its feet and stumbled on.

All the way back to its master it went. All the while the solemn word echoing in its ears, the monstrous sound not letting it rest until it had gotten to Vlandrax. The words ravished the sloth constantly. Never ceasing, never letting up, never leaving its nightmares. The one phrase that it would remember for the rest of its life: "Ralaeicoshooa ila cae."

Raifen I am.

Raifen picked himself up off the dirt and could still hear the remnants of what he had just heard. He could still hear the sound echoing through the tunnels as he walked back to his uncle and Clatistook. The one phrase he had kept uttering over and over and over again. He had been screaming it and had awakened something inside himself that he never knew was there. He wasn't sure what it was but it had done the job. The sloth had gone running away. He had discovered the creature's name when the power inside him had released. It had showed him his enemy and told him everything about it that there was to know. Raifen was stunned by the truth of this creature, which he had found out. How it had suffered so much and had been transformed into this hideous creature through the Bringer of Death's trickery and the ever-growing hatred in its soul.

Raifen felt deeply sorry for this creature. He would find a way to heal it one day. He promised himself that. Ralaeicoshooa ila cae still rung in his head as he came in the abandoned room that he had left his uncle and Clatistook in a little earlier. They had long since gone, but Raifen sat for a while pondering the words he had spoken to the sloth.

Ralaeicoshooa ila cae. *Raifen I am.*

What was the meaning of these words? Why had he spoken them? What had caused him to do so? He had too many questions that needed answers. He wished he knew all of them, but he knew that in time he would see.

A few minutes later after Seraph and Clatistook had gone through the other tunnel and through a secret passageway heading the other direction and opened into a ravine next to a small stream. Raifen had emerged through the hole. Seraph ran to him and hugged him tightly.

"Thank goodness. I was worried about you. You had me and Clatistook worried there for awhile."

Clatistook was huddled in the darkness next to a tree. He just stared sightlessly at Raifen. He knew Raifen was beginning to understand. And he would be there to help him. He would make sure of that. Raifen made his way over to where Clatistook was standing and stared into his eyes.

"I did it," Raifen said.

Clatistook nodded his head. Raifen seemed to be satisfied with that and went on and sat down on a log next to the water. He peered into the cool liquid and saw his reflection shining back at him. His face was more worn than the last time he had seen his appearance, but this time there shown something else, something that wasn't there before. He could see the light hue of color shining through his eyes, a mysterious presence that he did not completely understand. He could feel the energy flowing through his veins, moving from his toes to his legs, to his fingers and then his arms and back to his head and then replenishing in the source of its energy: the heart. He felt lighter, stronger, much more alive than he had ever felt. He liked this feeling, but he was cautious at the same time.

"I think we should go," Raifen finally decided.

"Follow me. I'll take us to the land that has been kept hidden from all unwanted eyes," Clatistook grinned.

Raifen fell back in line behind Clatistook and his uncle. Raifen wanted to be by himself for the time being. He needed some time to think about some things that were on his mind. Raifen saw that Seraph had a questioning and concerned look on his face, but didn't say anything to him and instead turned and followed Clatistook. There would be plenty of time for him to talk to Seraph and Raifen knew Seraph knew that. The mystery of the Nazracs' homeland would soon be revealed. The thought excited Raifen. He couldn't wait.

PEACE OF MIND

latistook stopped after awhile to settle down for camp to rest for the night. They had been traveling for a few hours now and he could feel that they needed a rest, himself included. He wasn't as young as he had been. His bones ached and his muscles were beginning to get sore.

"We'll make camp here for the night. I think we will be alright for awhile. We will continue in the morning. I suggest in the meantime you get some much needed rest," Clatistook smiled at Raifen when he spoke these last words. "You especially Raifen, there are many more truths yet to unfold for you. You'll need your rest for the tasks that await you."

And with those last comments, Clatistook plopped down on the ground and went to sleep. He had fallen asleep so fast that Raifen had almost thought he was faking it. If so, he didn't know. He left Clatistook to his dreams for now and took his advice to get some sleep.

Raifen walked over to where his uncle was getting ready for bed. Seraph had gotten a small fire cooking and was now setting up his blanket for the night. Raifen went out into the woods and found some more wood for the fire. It felt peaceful being out in the woods underneath the moon in the night sky. He felt a different tune this night. It felt as if the earth were at peace too. Raifen knew it was strange, but that's what it felt like. When he got back to the camp, Seraph was already asleep. He built up the fire and laid some big logs around the outside of the flames and built up a small fort of dirt to keep the fire in place. He put some more wood on the fire, enough to last them the night. He laid his blankets on the ground a few feet away from his uncle and settled down for the night. He laid there for a few moments before falling asleep. He thought of everything that had taken place that day and how now here he was. He was thankful. He smiled in spite of himself and then fell asleep. He would get a good rest this night, something that he wouldn't always get in the near future.

Ten feet away Clatistook laid underneath his blankets watching Raifen as he built up the fire and fixed his bed and then had fallen asleep. He could sense something had happened in the tunnels when Raifen had left. He just wasn't exactly sure what it was yet. He had heard the words that were spoken. Not as clear and focused as it would have been if he were there when they were spoken, but nonetheless, he could interpret them. They had more meaning than what he suspected Raifen understood. It would be awhile until he actually understood enough to make a big enough difference, but he was getting closer. He would make sure Raifen didn't learn too much, too fast. He would make sure things happened for a reason and that little at a time Raifen would begin to understand.

A PLEASED CONSPIRACY

eddrox was disturbed by the way the room made him feel. He had already seen odd ornaments on the walls: old paintings and wood carvings of animals decorated the shelves. He had the weird feeling he was being watched, if he only knew the truth in that statement. He walked over to the door that had been bolted shut sometime earlier when he was asleep. He had tried countless times to break it down but it proved too strong. His body was wearing out from banging on it. His hands and shoulders were turning raw under their touch. A few places the skin had ripped and blood had flowed, but was now long since dried up. Heddrox had decided not to bother with the door any longer. He spent his time doing something much more constructive: devising a plan of escape.

His chance would soon come but he had not foreseen the choice he would make. Heddrox was sitting on the bed pretending to be interested in one of the decorations on the wall when the door slid open. He had predicted this would happen and he was prepared. He had devised a plan that he meant to take in affect as soon as someone came to see him. His luck had finally paid off. His back was turned facing the door. He waited patiently for the person to come closer. He strained his ears to hear any sound of movement, but he heard nothing. Was he imagining that the door had come open? Had he made himself believe that his chance of escape had finally come? Heddrox wasn't sure, but he would wait a little longer to make sure. He heard a strange hissing noise to the right of him. He pretended he didn't hear. He heard it again, except it came from his left this time. He ignored that one too. A silence fell over the room. Perspiration began to flow down his forehead, cloaking his vision. The silence was broken by the hissing noise yet again. This time it was all around him. He couldn't take it any longer. He spun around ready to spring for the door and make his escape. On his way to turn his head, a poisonous snake shot out at him. It nearly got him, but he had made a last minute maneuver to avoid its piercing fangs. He rolled off the bed and began to crawl to the door. The hissing noise came from behind him now and he turned to see snakes slithering after him from all directions. His heart froze in place. His muscles tensed up and he choked on his breath. There were hundreds of them. The snakes were getting closer now. Their mouths opened wide with an anticipated hunger. He looked around for anything he could use as a weapon against these demons. He noticed a small desk a few feet away and he made for it. The snakes seemed to know his motives and hissed with defiance. Heddrox grabbed the desk and tore it from the wall and used it as a boundary between him and the snakes. The snakes whipped their tails frantically at the desk, biting and tearing the wood from the desk. He had a moment of time to get his bearings and then the snakes were crawling along the sides of the desk. He stumbled away. Crashing into the far corner of the room, he had to get to the door. If only he could get to it then he would be safe. He tried desperately to think of a plan. He had none. He fumbled in his clothes

MATTHEW THRUSH

for any weapon he might have, but soon found out that all his weapons were gone. They must have taken them from me, he thought to himself. His mind swung. His fingers were sweating now and he could hardly focus. A pain shot up from his leg. He looked down in horror to see a snake slithering in for its next attack. He kicked earnestly at it, sending it scurrying away. He had to get out of here and fast. He could feel his leg going numb. Once he lost all feeling to it, he would be in big trouble. His vision was beginning to go hazy. He could feel the poison making its course through his system. He hadn't much time. He knew he must do something fast or he would be finished. The thought of him passing out on the floor with all these monstrous snakes so close made his stomach crawl. He clawed at his pockets, hoping they might have missed something. There was nothing. All his pockets were empty. His fear arose then to the next volume. He was going to die here. This wasn't how he had imagined him going. No, he was not going to go like this. He was thinking about what his next move would be when his fingers fell upon an unexpected source of hope. In his shoe, underneath the sole, his fingers came in contact with his salvation. It was the *Cleakersao* elixir. He had been planning on using it on a special occasion. He figured this was as good a time as any. He wretched it out from his boot and looked at the clear crystalline tube protecting the valuable contents inside.

It was a darkness enhancer. When used it would cast a deep black over everything in its path, causing an utter darkness to fill the space. Only the user could see. His eyes peered into the tube at the silver outline of silky fibers in the dark liquid. He felt bad using it now, it seemed it was a waste of a perfectly good potion, but if he were to survive another day he would have to use it. He made up his mind. He pulled the cork from the tube and drank the contents. He dropped the container on the floor. The glass broke instantly and shattered in all different directions.

F rom another room, Essabella was watching the scene unravel as Heddrox fought to stay alive. He had already been bitten once. It wouldn't be long now until the poison sank in and finished the job. In truth, she was disappointed that such a skilled man as Heddrox would fail in such a task as this. She had thought him much more resourceful and able to get out of anything. That's what everyone said at least, "The untouchable and able-to-get-out-of-any-mess Heddrox."

He was widely known around the lands and was greatly feared and for good reason. He had killed many men and all for the sake of money. It was all disappointing to Essabella. She felt it was a waste of someone with his skills and talents to just throw it away doing un-meaningful tasks. She had expected him to get out of this instance quite easily. It was beginning to prove otherwise.

Heddrox had been in the room for five days already, unable to get out. She had grown tired of watching him break his body pounding against the door. She decided to take a different course. She had opened the door from the outside, and poured in the deadly snakes. They were called the Arachnefiees for their poison was to be of ten times that of the most poisonous arachnids. A gruesome death if one had the leisure of experiencing.

Essabella turned her eyes from the scene, unable to watch the outcome. She had been attracted to Heddrox in a way that seemed mysterious. When she turned her face, expecting to hear the ending screams of his agony, she was surprised to find that they didn't come. She frowned. Maybe Heddrox would prove himself after all. She turned and her eyes went white at the scene.

The room went black. A deep and unseeing cloud filled the room, sucking in all the features of the room and everything in it, disappearing from sight. Heddrox's throat still burned. He had not expected the sensations he was feeling now. His whole body felt as if it were floating through the air. He felt weightless. He couldn't feel his heart beating anymore. He would have thought himself dead if not for the continuous hissing close by. He could see the snakes now, all slithering about blindly. He grinned. He kicked at the snakes viciously. Sending them sailing through the darkness and hitting the wall on the other side of the room. Heddrox smashed at the snakes, trying to kill as many as he could. The snakes were disoriented and tried to flee. Heddrox was too fast for them. He stopped their escape and devoured them with his wrath. Oh, how he hated snakes! Especially these snakes that had tried to kill him. His anger began to subside after a few minutes and he remembered his present state. He looked up. The door was still ajar. He made for it. He stood by the door for an instant to look back at the scene unfolding in the room and then left.

Essabella was pleased at what she was seeing. Or what she wasn't seeing. It seemed Heddrox had a few tricks up his sleeves after all. She listened intently to the sounds coming from the room—the invisible room. Something was happening in there. She hoped it was what she had wanted from the start. She got up and left her crystal ball and headed toward the room. She had to find out what the outcome was. Her body shook with anticipation. How pleased she would be if it were true.

A MYSTERIOUS FIND

eddrox tumbled to the earth. Twigs and dirt flew in his eyes and mouth and he coughed on the gagging particles. His hair was in his face and he drew it back with his hands. Braiding the fine silk on his head to keep from blocking his visibility, Heddrox pondered the landscape.

"Hello," called Heddrox, choking on the rough, dry feeling in his throat.

The sound echoed the forest walls.

Heddrox looked around for a means of escape, but found none available. Trees upon trees surrounded him. He was trapped. He had left one dungeon for another. Heddrox thought when he left the room, through the solid door, that he was escaping the deathly snakes that bound it. But he only brought himself to another locked chamber: the woods. Heddrox stumbled over his feet, dragging his left leg like a dead carcass. It stung with the snake's venom. The poison was making its course to his heart. He could feel it running through his veins. He had to get help and fast.

"Hello? Hello? Anyone out there?" cried Heddrox.

No answer. The trees blew in the evening breeze, a soft murmur of twigs snapping with the combining force of the branches twisting amongst one another. The earth was hard beneath Heddrox's feet, a gentle reminder of the strength that harvested in the depths. An off-beat rhythm of thumps shot through the ground. Heddrox's feet stammered about.

Heddrox's vision began to weaken. The trees swayed back and forth, mixing colors and forming, combining into one. The ground rocked and beat up and down. Heddrox's head ached with ensuing pain, shooting vibrations and chills up and down his spine. Heddrox wavered in his step, only for a few seconds then fell. The rotating colors of the forest disappeared with the closing of his eyes, transforming into a different color, a new nausea: blackness. The edge of wakefulness was close by and Heddrox went over.

Twigs snapped and creaked as the figure wobbled through the forest. The sun was up, but thick overhanging branches of the Tirster Forest were too much. The forest floor was rather dark, a painted gray from the lack of sunlight. There was hardly any foliage on the ground, but plenty of rough dirt and small patches of grass, but dead grass at that. The whole outlook seemed rather pale and blank. The figure was used to the way the woods looked and didn't bother much. It had been many years since the figure had been outside these firm and tall confined walls, too long indeed. The years could be felt with each passing step the figure took. The steps were more ragged and unstable. The cloaked figure was going about its evening walk looking for wood when it came upon a body. Although the face looked deathly pale and the form lifeless, the figure couldn't help but notice how handsome he was. The dark eyebrows that shadowed his eyes, the sharp-edged and firm cheekbones that hung like strong pillars, and the soft curved nose that ended at the tip of those delicious lips caused emotion to stir within the figure. Small, old hands reached out and took hold of one of the well-shaped arms of the body. It felt cold to the touch. Fear ranked through the blood of this hooded person and it quickly scurried away, dragging the body behind it.

ℌeddrox opened his eyes. After blinking several times, without any luck clearing the fog that lingered, he finally managed to see. It must still be dark, he thought. He twisted around to lie on his back. His eyes were sealed with plaster and he could barely make out his surroundings. He rubbed his eyes. The visibility was better, but not all that good still. He peered through the shrouded mist and slowly and gradually began to spot things, his eyes growing accustomed to the darkness. Heddrox was unsure of his eyes, for he saw things as if he were in some room. He couldn't be in a room. He had fallen in the woods? It was all too strange for him. An ache was bothering him considerably and he reached down to feel where it was manifesting.

His fingers grazed over a gooey substance just under the calf muscle. His hand retracted on impulse. Afraid for the worse he reached down again to get a better feel. He struck moisture again and the oozing substance slid between his fingers. It was sticky and almost solid feeling. He smelled it and then tasted it. Iron? It tasted like iron, but it couldn't be. Heddrox swayed into unconsciousness and fell back down on the cot. His hand fell over the edge, the red liquid dripped to the floor. It hadn't been a dream after all.

THE HERBALIST

The old figure walked in and saw the body still unconscious. It had moved. It saw the arm dangling off the edge of the table. There was a reddish substance dripping from one of its fingers. It grimaced as it saw the puddle of blood lying pooled on the wood floor. It quietly cleaned the hand of the blood and wiped up the liquid from the floor as well. It was good the body was asleep. It had worried the figure for quite some time that he wouldn't make it. The figure had done everything in its power and skill to heal the wound. It had been a gruesome scene once it had cut open the pant leg to reveal a rather nasty looking infection. The figure had done some tests and soon found out that it had been a bite, a poisonous one. It tried countless antidotes, but nothing seemed to work.

The man had a severe fever and it refused to break. The figure was running out of time and medicines. It unlocked the hidden wall and the door swung open. Inside were rows and rows of herbs, ingredients, medicines. Anything one could think of was there. It took many years for the figure to obtain its precious collection. It was far from being complete, but it was rather remarkable at the least. The figure quickly scanned the shelves for what it was looking for. Finally spotting the small capsule, it trotted back over to the unconscious body. The figure looked down at the handsome face. The thought that it might never be seen again made the figure terribly sad. It unfastened the corkscrew from the lip of the container and poured a little in a small stewing pot nearby. Once the fluid touched, the black liquid shot out and scurried about the pan's bottom instantly. It sought to escape. The hunched over figure poured something else in the pot and it suddenly hissed. The body behind it moaned.

The figure had to hurry or it would be too late. It added a small herb to the mix and a gentle billow of smoke curled toward the ceiling. The figure took a small portion of the liquid, using a small device to carry it over to the body. It slowly poured the contents of the potion into the mouth of the dying man. The body instantly started to spasm out of control. The figure hurried to hold down the body. It barely could hold on and was about to be thrown back from the mighty force of the spasm when it began to die down. The body laid still after a few moments. The potion was doing the trick. Satisfied, the figure went over and poured the rest of the dark liquid into a vial. After topping it with a lid, the figure sat down. The rocking chair squeaked softly as the hinges swung back and forth. The figure sat there, watching the body as it fought the ensuing battle that was raging within. It didn't know if the antidote would work. It might have been too late. Only time would tell.

AS ONE COMBINED

He tossed and turned violently in his sleep. The dream was terrible. He awoke with a shout. He peered around the camp where they were sleeping. Seraph and Clatistook were still sound asleep. He was surprised the shout didn't wake either of them. It must have been in the dream. Sweat dripped and soaked his whole body. His trousers and linen shirt were drenched. The perspiration foamed on his brow and his hair was matted. Raifen laid back down after waking up from the nightmare. It was still dark, but he could see the faint glow of the sunrise climbing over the mountain coast. They had been traveling for three weeks now and they had long since left the city of Blasa. Clatistook had urged them that they would stay as close to the mountainside as possible without being dragged into the harsh climate of the Blasandi Desert. Clatistook had said that would be a terrible mistake on their parts if they went through that barren wasteland. They would have soon run out of water and have had no choice but to turn back around. That was not an option. Raifen had slept fine the previous nights earlier on in the journey. But ever since he had come into contact with the thing that called itself the sloth, things had been different. He had strange feelings nonstop. As they traveled, he became more and more distant from his uncle and Clatistook. They seemed oblivious of it, but Raifen knew his uncle was being crushed. But, he couldn't help it. It wasn't like he was doing it on purpose. He didn't even know why it seemed things were coming to

MATTHEW THRUSH

how they were. He just knew that something unnatural was happening. And he couldn't do anything to stop it. *Yet.*

Raifen tumbled back down onto the earth. He had long since cast his blanket aside, for it was way too hot, even in the night and off the edge of the desert. Though it was dark, there seemed to be no breeze that existed, at least where they were for that matter. There was no refuge from the dying heat. The desert was undiminished and never wavered in its onslaught attack on their spirits. Raifen had already become angered countless times and had voiced his aggressions. Clatistook had remained silent for days now. And Raifen and his uncle's relationship was crumbling. Something had to be done or it might be too late to salvage their family bond. Raifen found himself regretting ever leaving Sol. He missed his home, although he constantly had to remind himself that he had to leave. He had to grumble about with that fact and it proved a heavy and tiresome load, which got heavier and thicker as the days transgressed. The thoughts ran about his mind. He could do nothing to halt their endless bickering. He finally gave up and went back to sleep. He was no safer there, in his dreams, than he was in the daylight, wide awake. It seemed there was no escaping them.

Raifen was the first to wake up. It seemed it was beginning to be a normal everyday occurrence. He quietly gathered his stuff together, violently shoving his thin sheet into his pack. He got up and walked about the forest's edge to try and walk off some of his aggressions. Every so often he would stop and pick up a piece of abandoned wood off the ground. There was not much to be found on the far side of the mountain that lay next to the desert, of which he stood now. But, as if to heighten his spirits just a little, there came a soft whistle through the streaming glare of the morning sun. And to make matters seemingly better and more pleasant, there began to blow a soft and cooling breeze from the east.

Raifen couldn't help but crack a smile. Something he hadn't done for over a week now. He kept on walking, glad finally that there was some kind of refuge from the heat. He hadn't gone much farther when he heard the whistle again. This time it was closer than before. He tried to whistle back but found his mouth too parched. He cursed the heat. He continued and soon came upon a small ravine. The sound of drifting water was the most pleasant thing Raifen had heard in a long time, exempting the soft whistle of a few minutes ago. Raifen ran to the sound and found it shortly after going about thirty feet and climbing through a short web of trees.

Raifen plunged his face and hands into the cool liquid. The feeling of water on his lips and face sparked an inner joy and peace. He quickly drank as much water as he could, using his hands in a cupped position. He then took out his canteen and filled it up too. Satisfied and refreshed, he laid next to a tree. He closed his eyes, something that finally felt good. Time ceased to exist and his thoughts roamed through happier tendencies. A good amount of time went by and he was brought back to reality with the sharp cry just above him. His eyes shot open and he looked around to see what had made the noise. He was unsure whether or not it had really been a noise he had heard or if it had just been his imagination.

He closed his eyes again, thinking it must have been his imagination, when he heard it again. He stood up and tried, with no success, to peer into the depths of the tree he was just sitting under. It appeared that was where the noise was coming from. He slowly crept closer, all the while looking at the branches of the tree for any signs of movement. He quit his jostling and went to that area. But once there, the whistle came from behind him then.

Spinning around, confused, Raifen looked around for where it had come from. It whistled again and this time it was in another tree, farther away. Raifen casually walked toward it. The whistle seemed to be floating off the breeze, masking where its true location was. Raifen had trouble finding where it had gone. He went from tree to tree, following the sound. He had found a small crossing at the bank of a small ravine and made way to the other side. He was now deep into the abiding forest edge when the whistle stopped and blurted one final tune. Silence rained for a long time. An eternity. His surroundings were unclear and he began to panic. He didn't know which way to go. He was lost. The thought creased his inner turmoil of earlier and it sprang back to life his frustration and temper. Just when he was about to explode, the sharp cry of the creature sounded and out of a tree ahead shot the most beautiful bird Raifen had ever seen. It was pitch black, with a hint of blue and red masking its stomach and spreading a greenish hue toward its black wings. It was a small bird, only about the size of a sparrow, but it commanded Raifen's attention with ease. It drifted and flew about the forest in countless semi-circles. Raifen was dizzy trying to follow its every move. It was completely graceful and smooth in its approach. Raifen didn't even notice it coming closer to him until it had landed on his arm. The small bird perched itself on his forearm and looked up at him. It squeaked, causing Raifen to flinch, but then to smile.

"Hi there little fella. How you doing?" spoke Raifen. "Where'd you come from?"

The bird seemed oblivious to his words and just stared up at him. Raifen stroked its wings and body with his finger. Raifen was surprised that it let him. He felt an awkward bond with this little creature of the wood. It seemed he was a part of it and it a part of him in the same. Raifen went to stroke it again, but failed.

"Hello Raifen," it suddenly spoke. Its voice was a soft humming sound. Raifen was shocked, but thrilled at the same time.

"Hello," he answered. He couldn't believe he was talking to a bird. First he talks to trees and now a bird. What's next, a rock?

"Yes," the bird answered him.

"Yes, what?" he asked, but seemingly already knowing what the answer was.

"Yes to your question," it sang.

Raifen was awestruck. Not only could he talk with this little bird, but now it could hear his thoughts, too. It was weird.

"How come I can talk to you?" asked Raifen, hoping to clear his mind a little of this strange confusion that had sprung up. The bird seemed to smile at him. Though there were no characteristics identifiable of it being able to do so.

"Because," it began, "all creatures can."

"But that doesn't answer my question," protested Raifen.

"No," it soothingly said.

"No it doesn't. I'm a human. You're a bird."

"Yes," it hummed, still smiling.

"Exactly, by all laws of nature I shouldn't be able to talk to you," stated Raifen.

"We do not consist with the normal laws of nature," it fluttered.

"You are not of the normal spiral of things," the bird continued. "So, you can do things that others shall never be able to do. Like talk to me," it chirped with a gleeful grin.

Raifen didn't understand.

"And what spiral or realm am I in then?" asked Raifen.

"Yours," it answered.

"Mine?" stated Raifen.

"Yes."

"I don't understand."

There was a snapping of twigs behind Raifen and he turned. Someone was coming. He turned back to face the bird.

"In time you will find, the answers you seek are out of reach from the blind. But, in action, you shall come to a conclusion that will identify your confusion that might lead to your approving satisfaction."

With those words uttered, the bird took flight and

disappeared into the trees once more, leaving Raifen completely confused.

"Raifen. There you are. You had us worried."

Raifen turned around. It was Clatistook. He looked around and had a mischievous grin on his face.

"It seems you have found the Tome of the Flutters," stated Clatistook.

Raifen didn't answer. The words of the bird still played in his head. A blank expression covered his face. Clatistook didn't bother though. It seemed he knew more of what was happening then he wished to let on.

"Is this what this place is called," he stammered, more to himself.

"Yes," answered Clatistook, as if Raifen had asked him the question. Raifen nodded with apprehension.

"Come," began Clatistook, "let's get back to the camp. We need to be going."

He ushered with his hand and began to walk the way he had come. Raifen hesitated, and then followed. The trees disappeared behind him as they came into the vast mouth of the desert. Seraph was leaning over the fire cooking something in a stew pot. The smell wafted in the air and caught Raifen in the nose. His stomach growled. He didn't realize how hungry he was. He walked over to his uncle and sat down next to him.

"You hungry?" asked Seraph, ignoring the fact that his nephew had been gone when he and Clatistook woke up. Though he was extremely worried, he knew deep down that Raifen would be all right. Clatistook had said so. And so far, Seraph believed him to be correct.

"Starving," replied Raifen. "What are you cooking?" He tried to look over the pot to see what his uncle was cooking up.

"Just a little something to quench our hunger for awhile," Seraph grinned. "It's some beef stew with some vegetables that I was able to salvage from the little tunnel adventure we had." He placed a knowing smile Raifen's way. Raifen was thankful. Seraph soon handed Raifen a bowl full of steaming roast and vegetables. Shortly after, he poured himself and Clatistook a bowl as well. The three of them sat there in silence, eating their meal. All three knew that they had a long day ahead of them and they absorbed as much energy as they could. Talking could be used as a wasteful act. Raifen soon forgot about his little encounter with the bird in the woods. Happy to be eating and on his way, nothing else mattered at the moment. He had plenty of time in the future to think of what happened. For now, he concentrated on eating. Something he loved doing more than almost anything else.

ANSWERS—OR NOT

I t had been four days now since the antidote was administered to the body. It appeared to the satisfaction of the figure keeping close watch over it that he was beginning to get well. The potion was doing its job. It was only a matter of time before he would wake up again. And when he did, the figure had some questions to ask him. There had been no telling what would happen to the man lying on the table when the potion was given. It was a very powerful liquid, the only one of its kind. It was known to not even exist. But that was of course false, since the figure had it. But through means that were far more deadly than the poison that had infected the body. It would be another day or two before he would finally wake up concluded the figure. And so, it pulled back on its hood and walked out of the little house. There was a small fire in the chimney to keep the house warm while it was gone.

The man would be all right. There was nothing else it could do but wait, and besides, it had some other matters to tend to. Especially if what it thought were true about this one. In that case it hurried quickly through the paths of trees to the destination of its choice. The cave loomed out of the rock up ahead. The darkness of its depths crept out with its hungry arms. The figure disappeared within the confined walls of the rock. The dark swallowed it whole. Anxious still for more and therefore continued on its senseless ambition to rule the world around it. It would succeed every so often for a few hours, but then its rival, light,

MATTHEW THRUSH

would come back and shun it back to its fortress, only to wait and gain its strength for another attempt.

The cave was dense and swollen with the stink of death. The figure knew what happened in these caves, and of what lived in them, too. No, it wasn't just the dark that lived here. Something more foul used it as its slave of mischief. Only to mask the true substance that lay within the walls of the mountain. The figure fumbled with something in its pocket then finally drew it out. It poured some on a stick and it instantly alighted with a flame of bright light. Now with one of the problems taken care of, it only needed to worry about one more. It was never a pleasing experience to seek the wisdom of the Drom. The Drom was the only one of its kind. A *drom*, itself, was the type of species and name the creature gave itself. It was full of wisdom and knowledge of everything about the land and what went on in it. If there was something someone wanted to know, the Drom was the thing to seek. But one had to know the password first. And it often came with a high price. But, the figure needed answers and the Drom was sure to have them, even if it would cost some kind of payment. The figure knew the rules of the game and was willing to pay in full whatever it cost. Though, if it had known what it would pay for this next little information, it might have never entered the cave again.

The figure slowly maneuvered through the cave's tunnel system. It had been years since it had been here and its memory wasn't as good as it used to be. Many times it became lost and had to retrace its steps to where it had come from. This went on for hours before it finally knew something was wrong. The cave had changed. Frustrated that it hadn't realized sooner and saved itself the trouble of walking around aimlessly it sat down on a rock nearby. It slowly began to catch its breath and then decided to do what it knew all along that it would have to do. Although it wished it wouldn't have to. The time of peace was over. Now was time to call the Drom. The memory was a little hazy but it finally came to it. It knocked the code on the wall. It did so on every wall that surrounded it. It was the custom to do so if you were seeking refuge or wisdom from the Drom.

Few had ever succeeded and the figure had learned the skill from its former master who had found the secret *thing*. The figure waited a few moments then repeated the task. It continued this routine three times more, stopping and listening after each pass to make the total of five knockings that it took. All there was now to do was wait. Something the figure was used to doing. But right now, it lacked the normal intensity of patience. The figure thought it heard something. The figure was getting a little more doubtful as the seconds passed and turned into minutes, possibly hours. Finally the figure gave up and decided to try again later. The Drom must not be in the mountain at the time, though the figure knew of no other time that it had left its sanctuary of rock. That was uncommon and brought a strange nervousness to the figure's mind. The figure began the endless journey of getting back out.

The Drom watched from the safety of the darkness. The figure had gotten the secret knock correct, but it wasn't about to reveal itself yet. It was curious as to how this being knew its code. The Drom had been clever as to how it had made up the code that it thought no one or thing would ever be able to find its secret. The Drom was mistaken years back and awakened from its keep sleep by the knocking. Something or someone had been tapping the code. The code the Drom thought impossible to break. It had been full of rage at this prospect but soon became curious as to how it had been done instead. It had gone then and that was when it had met the first Yul. As that was what the man was called. The man had been old as the Drom could tell by scanning him with its nocturnal eyes, but it could feel that the man was much younger and stronger than his appearance led it to believe. The Drom had dropped right out from the crack in the ceiling that was its exit and landed right in front of the man. Though the Drom was powerful, it still was uncertain of the secrets and powers that dwelled within the confines of the man's body. With no other sign of how powerful it was than the fact of it being able to break the hardest code there ever was made. That alone showed the Drom that this one was not one to take lightly.

"Who dare awaken me from my sleep?" the Drom asked. Its voice shook the walls of the cave with a loud rumble. The voice was full of power and control. It echoed off the stone and bounced about. It spoke again, this time with a thunderous roar.

The man had not even flinched. He merely stepped closer to the sound. This sign of power took the Drom aback; the voice of death didn't even brush the surface of the man's flesh. There was something different and unusual about this one. The Drom had wanted to find out its source of so much obvious power and hopefully bring him into his grasp. It knew it had to have some extreme power or gift, for death was not held off lightly. It took someone of great skill to do so. Apparently the man did.

"Who are you?" hissed the Drom.

"I am Yul," answered the man flatly.

The Drom twisted its head sideways. It hissed with pleasure.

"I know of no Yul. And I know all," spoke the Drom.

The man shrugged his shoulders.

"You must not know as much as you think," answered the man.

The Drom growled and roared, tearing layers of rock away from the walls of the mountain with its mighty hands.

"You lie!" yelled the Drom.

The man hadn't moved from the position he was in. The Drom was getting more angry than curious now. Drom hated calm. Drom hated courage. And Drom hated life the most. Who was this man? Why was he here? What power did he wield, Drom wondered. The Drom needed some answers and he wanted them now.

"Who are you?" the Drom asked again.

The man replied, "I am Yul."

"What is Yul?" thundered Drom.

"I am," briskly answered the man.

The Drom couldn't take it any longer. Not only was

this man not scared of him, but he now was toying with him. The Drom hated the fact that he couldn't control this man and make him dread ever being here. The thought riveted its mind. Its mind clouded with anger and malice and hate. The man seemed to be enjoying himself. He couldn't help suppress a small grin. The man finally spoke up.

"I am in need of your advice," stated the man. He waited to make sure the Drom had heard him. He took the absence of falling rock as it was listening.

"I need to know what you know," stated the man. "I need the knowledge of the land."

The statements weren't questions, but straightforward remarks, as if they were a command. The Drom wasn't sure what the man had meant, but took it as if he were asking him instead of demanding him.

The man couldn't be that stupid. Could he? Or was he really that powerful, he thought.

"What knowledge do you seek with questioning?" hissed the Drom with displeasure.

"I need to know the history of the land. I need to know its secrets, its failures and its successes. I need to know everything there is to know about what lies in this land and in the land that surrounds it across the seas," the man said.

"What makes you think I will give it to you?" growled the Drom, daring the man to do something foolish. The Drom got his wish.

"I know you will," started the man, "because you have no other choice."

This last statement pleased the Drom in the fact that it finally allowed him to have a reason to hate this man, but also, to anger him with the man's obvious cockiness. Who did this man think he was? Who was he to just walk right in and demand whatever he wanted from the Drom?

"You can't demand anything from me!" hissed the Drom. "Do you know who I am, boy?" asked the Drom, clearly using the term *boy* to try and get the man worked up.

The man just stood there for a moment before replying.

"I am a boy in the sense of years when compared to the enormity of years you have dwelled on this land. But by using *boy* you dare to question my authority…" the man left the sentence hanging. He pointed a finger at the Drom. The Drom watched, readying itself to spring and devour this menace.

"You will obey me or you shall die!" the man said.

Although the Drom was furious and willed himself to lunge at this defiled man, devour and crush him with his mighty claws, it couldn't. The Drom was even more infuriated when it seemed he was shackled to the spot it was standing. Try all he might, the Drom couldn't move a muscle. It yelled of defiance and hatred, but to no array. The Drom glared at the smirk that was now forming on the man's face.

"It seems you have no choice," said the man. "Now, where was I? Oh yes. *The land.*"

The Drom told everything. The words and knowledge that it held so sacred was absorbed from him. There was nothing it could do. The reality of what was happening never took full root. *Who was this man? What was he?*

Where did he come from? The Drom told the man everything there was to know about the Land of Forlar. Then about the different seas and how they moved and blew and what transpired there, even the different creatures that dwelled in different places on the land. It told every secret there was. And it hated the man for it. All sense of self was lost in a matter of moments. The Drom felt depleted and empty. It felt assaulted. And it would be right in that conclusion. It was assaulted. And not by any ordinary person either. The Drom couldn't help but say it.

"He is Yul."

The Drom came back to the present state and of the situation at hand. The memories of the past were meant to be remembered, but not to be dwelled on too much or they would consume you. Apparently they had already done the job. The Drom was ruled now by the past. Not of death and anger. But anger and hate for the things that transpired. One moment in particular, and the memory of that time frustrated the Drom and it couldn't suppress its quietness any longer. Just when the figure was about to leave the room down a tunnel that was sure to hinder it more hours of aimless wondering, the Drom spoke.

"What be your reason for waking me?" he growled. It was hesitant more so this time. The memory of what happened the last time all too closely on his mind. The figure turned around and walked back into the room. It stood a few feet from the Drom. It clearly couldn't see it for it looked around with the look of searching.

"Who are you?" asked the Drom, to find out who and

what this person was. Hoping it wasn't the one of before, though it already knew it wasn't. This one hobbled and had a limp. The other did not. This one as the Drom could now feel had some fear or doubt. That was good. The Drom grew more anticipative. The figure hesitated before speaking. Another good sign concluded the Drom.

"I need your help," stated the figure, its voice shaking. The Drom laughed within. This person was pathetic. But, as the Drom had learned, appearances could be deceiving. If for no other reason to hold a doubt about this person, it was the fact as well that it had known the code, thus making it the second to ever do so. The Drom was careful, but not overly so.

"What help do you seek?" rumbled the Drom.

"I have need for answers," said the figure.

"What is it that you need answering for?" asked the Drom, just wanting to go back to its den and sleep for another couple hundred years. Hopefully it would have that long before another person came that could break his code and wake him up.

"I have someone," the figured stated. "Someone that might interest you."

The Drom was passive.

"I have the heir of Yul."

The words stung the Drom. The word. The same menacing word that had haunted it for hundreds of years now spurred new hatred and anger in his foul blood.

"What about the Yul," it growled.

The figure clearly realized it had struck a wrong note and backed up immediately.

"I have his heir," it stated again.

"What do you mean?" hissed the Drom.

"His son. I have him."

The Drom's first reaction was hate and anger. But now, it had a new kind of feeling. One it had never really had before. *Revenge.*

"I didn't know the Yul had a son," stated the Drom, hating the usage of the word but knowing it was worth the risk.

"Neither did I. Or anyone else for that matter, but he did and I have him." spoke the figure eagerly.

"Where is this son at now?" asked the Drom, trying to sound as if it was of no importance. But it was all the importance in the world.

"Safe," the figure answered curtly.

"*Safe,*" hissed the Drom. "What do you mean *safe?*"

"He is being taken care of," was what the figure said.

The Drom hummed his tune of thought. It needed answers just like the figure needed his answers. The Drom quickly came up with a plan.

"Will you tell me what I need to know or not?" asked the figure. The change of control and bravery were enough to halt the Drom in his plan, but it soon decided to follow through.

"Yes," answered the Drom. "But only if you answer my question."

The figure seemed to be taken aback.

"I didn't know the Drom ever had questions? I thought it knew everything," stated the figure. The Drom was angered by this comment, but kept still and silent. There was no need to alert this person to his plan just yet.

"There is one thing I do not know," stated the Drom. "And I wish to know it."

The figure was curious as was expected from anyone who had knowledge enough to know the Drom never needed anything from anyone.

"Agreed?" hissed the Drom.

The figure hesitated. It was clearly debating in its head whether or not it was a good idea. Possibly whether or not it could trust the Drom. The Drom smiled at this thought. Of course the figure could trust him, but it didn't mean he would have trusted himself. The figure seemed to have reached a decision.

"Agreed," answered the figure.

"Good," hissed the Drom.

"I want my question answered first," stated the figure. "Or I will not answer yours."

The Drom couldn't help but applaud this action. It was obvious the Drom had underestimated this person. The second time he had ever done so. It would make sure it didn't again. The Drom nodded its head in agreement.

"Okay," began the figure. "Where do the Nazracs reside?"

The Drom thought it was going to get away with murder.

"Petipala," it answered shortly.

"I know that. How do I get there?" asked the figure.

The smile quickly faded away from the snarl of a mouth of the Drom. The Drom didn't know. The thought struck him over and over again. The Drom was flabbergasted and angry at the same time. Fumes of smoke shot out of his nostrils. His eyes burned red. He began to scratch and tear at the floor. The figure saw this change of stature and decided it was best to leave. While the Drom was fuming over something the figure quickly and quietly snuck away. The Drom didn't even know the figure had left. Nor did it care at the moment. It was full of hatred. Hatred towards the world and all the secrets it held. Hatred toward itself for not knowing and hatred for the Yul.

This last thought triggered the Drom. It turned to where the figure was, but found that it no longer was there anymore. The Drom looked about frantically. It was gone. The figure had left and the Drom hadn't even noticed. Its anger was too much. It exploded.

The figure now ran as fast as its disfigured leg would allow. Behind it some way off came the bellow of some volcano that just erupted. The figure knew that the Drom had finally realized the figure was gone. It couldn't believe it had gotten this far before the Drom reacted. The figure knew, as it was trained in Thalic, that the Drom hadn't known the answer to the question it had asked it. Thalic was a practice of breaking into the minds of others. It was a difficult thing to learn and do that many who tried ended up going mad. Oftentimes the most likely thing that would happen would be someone would die from the attempt. The figure had long since mastered this power and it used it well. Though the breakthrough was not as clear as the figure would have liked, it still got the picture. The Drom had no idea. The figure knew that was the time to leave. The figure was now almost to the exit of the cave. It could see the light shinning up ahead. The figure broke through the boundary of darkness and light. The feud still ranging between the two, it was obvious that light was winning. Which was to be expected since it was nearing the midday. The figure was shaken by the wave of power that shot from behind it. The entrance to the cave exploded with the same sound. As the figure continued to run as fast as its legs would allow, it heard what was now being yelled, at the top of the Drom's lungs would be a sure guess.

"Yul! Who is Yul?"

The figure broke through the first layer of foliage that blocked its way. The last thing that it heard come from behind it before all went silent was these words being screamed by the Drom:

"Who is the Yul? Who is the Yul? Who is the…"

The voice was shut off as the set of branches that the figure had just run through closed behind it, shutting off the sound and sentence. The words rang through the figure's mind as it raced away. Who is the Yul?

So that's what the Drom wanted to ask. A small grin crossed the figure's face. It was glad it hadn't told it. The figure knew of course who the Yul was. The figure was probably the only one who did know the truth.

Yul was Vlandrax Xen, the Bringer of Death. Her husband.

Herein lies the end of this book. The series
will continue with Raifen: *The Escape*.